The Betrayer

Born and bred in Bradford, Yorkshire, Domini Wiles lives with
her daughter and works as a poet/broadcaster for the local radio
station. She was educated to secondary school level, leaving a
little before her fifteenth birthday with no qualifications but a
great deal of ambition. Her first novel, written some eighteen
years ago, is still in its original, hand-written form, and over the
years she has experimented with numerous subjects and styles.
As a dialect poet, she has appeared on television and radio, and
many of her short stories have been published in national
magazines. Her first published novel, *Death Flight*, appeared in
1977. It was followed by *Skin Deep*.

Also by Domini Wiles
in Pan Books
Death Flight

Domini Wiles

The Betrayer

Pan Books in association with Collins

First published 1979 by William Collins Sons & Co. Ltd
This edition published 1981 by Pan Books Ltd,
Cavaye Place, London SW10 9PG
in association with William Collins Sons & Co. Ltd
© Domini Wiles 1979
ISBN 0 330 26280 7
Printed and bound in Great Britain by
Hazell Watson & Viney Ltd, Aylesbury, Bucks

one

Vince Wilder slid the pistols from the bag and placed them side by side in the glove compartment of the car. Then he licked his forefinger and rubbed it along the polished handle of the sawn-off shotgun, scowling at the small scratch which refused to be erased. It would have been a simple precaution to wrap the weapons separately before placing them in the canvas bag. He rubbed the scratch again, irritated by his own carelessness. Details mattered, however trivial. They had to. They added up to the finished product, and the way each one was handled might determine the outcome of the whole job. It would be too easy to overlook something seemingly insignificant and then find the rest of his plans set out of line because of it. One small scratch on the handle of his shotgun was not that important. What mattered was his own attention to detail. He was about to pull the biggest, the most crucial job of his career, and he couldn't afford to make mistakes.

The hired car pulled smoothly away from the kerb: a shabby, eight-year-old Ford which wouldn't attract enough attention to be remembered. He drove slowly, glancing sideways from time to time to make sure that the bag containing the shotgun was secure on the seat beside him. Instead of adopting the slouched comfort of his usual driving position, he sat well forward in his seat and gripped the wheel with both hands. He was not exactly nervous, certainly not scared, but the long weeks of waiting for the right time to move had keyed him up. It was a familiar sense of exhilaration that dried his mouth and tensed his muscles, giving him a sharp awareness of his body which was almost sensual. According to his contact, the diamond shipment was at last stashed away in the basement safe, illegal, uninsured, and virtually unprotected. Alone, it was worth over a quarter of a million dollars. If his contact had been feeding him the correct information, the whole job was worth twice that amount.

The men who were to help him were small-time, willing to

take risks for a few thousand in jewellery and whatever else they might be fortunate enough to find. He had offered the job to Kevin Rey, a man he knew to be capable of taking orders and getting on with a job without asking too many questions, and left it to him to hire a precautionary back-up man. The guns would ensure a smooth, quick operation with a minimum of resistance. It was that simple. The other two men would get their share, and Wilder himself would keep the contents of the basement safe. All they had been promised was a cut of the goods and cash which were kept in the shop. If they were fools enough to be satisfied with such small takings, he saw no reason to reward them with anything more. Noble gestures were not part of his nature, and as far as he was concerned, small-time thieves were only worth small-time pay-offs.

He parked the car on the opposite side of the street some one hundred yards from the jewellery shop. Even from that angle, he could clearly read the printed names of Lancing and Warwick above the front window. He checked his watch. Another half-hour to wait. A breeze from the open window cooled his face and carried the smells of a distant hot-dog stand into the car. He glanced at the shotgun and smiled, drumming his fingers on the edge of the steering wheel in a rhythmic tattoo. Across the street, something like half a million in cash and diamonds was sitting in the basement of a modest-looking shop, and it was his for the taking. With a sawn-off shotgun in his hand and two armed men to back him up, cleaning out Lancing and Warwick's was going to be easy.

Vince Wilder was thirty-four years old and obsessed with a desire to be rich. He craved the life-style, the possessions, the independence which came with wealth. He wanted respect and admiration. He wanted other men to look on him with envy, to hate him for his display of superiority. To him, money was everything. It superseded family status, which he had not been born to and natural talents, with which he did not consider himself blessed. It represented success and it brought with it unlimited power. To possess it in large quantities was the only ambition Wilder had ever known.

He tilted the rear-view mirror so that he could see his face.

A tendril of hair had fallen across his forehead, disturbed by the soft breeze. He eased it back in place with one gloved finger. He was a man who took great pride in his appearance, firmly believing that style and sophistication were the next best things to a large bank account. He bought expensive clothes and hand-made shoes, and he wore them with an elegance which was natural. A little over six feet tall, his dark eyes were framed by heavy lashes and his smile revealed near-perfect teeth. His features were even and unblemished, his silky brown hair so well cut that it seldom looked untidy. He was something of an athlete, keeping his body in good shape with plenty of sport and exercise. Like his clothes, his body was a status symbol, to be lovingly cared for and kept in perfect order.

It had taken much longer than he had anticipated to organize the diamond robbery, mostly due to the fact that his contact had been awaiting delivery of the special shipment of stones now in the safe. Its theft would seal off that particular route back at its source, a thing which Wilder much regretted. He would have appreciated the opportunity to tap the seam and perhaps expand the profits by taking it into a much bigger league. He had no way of knowing how big or how powerful the people might be who were already involved, at different stages, in the diamond run, but he certainly would have welcomed the chance to find out. According to his contact, Lancing and Warwick were systematically milking a very rich cow.

Wilder knew a great deal about the men he was going to rob, and his interest in them extended beyond the takings to the possible consequences of the robbery. Losing the diamond shipment would place them in one hell of a position, along with anyone else who happened to be involved in their deals. With the overseas agents screaming for payment, and the cash-paying customers demanding their goods, the outwardly respectable diamond merchants would be like a couple of fat steaks between two packs of hungry hounds. The prospect brought a smile of satisfaction to Wilder's face. It pleased him to think of them as his victims. It pleased him even more to think that he could break them so easily.

Max Lancing was the younger partner: aggressive, dynamic,

and obviously both brain and brawn behind the diamond run. He had entered the business as a high-class salesman, moving in the more sophisticated circles to sell his partner's very original pieces of jewellery to wealthy customers with an eye for exclusive design. In a few short years he had progressed from specialized salesman to undercover diamond merchant. The business was now a front for one of the richest of the small markets in uncut stones.

Wilder squinted at the neatly painted names on the front of the shop. It had not been easy to discover exactly what was going on behind the scenes of this legitimate business. Now that he was here, about to collect the rewards of his patience, he knew that all his scheming and conniving had been worthwhile.

He sat back and thought of Lancing, tall and broad, with the body of a thirty-year-old and the kind of craggy, weather-beaten features that were ageless. His energies extended to climbing mountains and his talents to speaking several languages. At forty-eight years of age, he was probably fitter, more successful, and more self-assured than Wilder would ever be. Ruining a bent old man like George Warwick would be little more than a consequence of the job, but bringing Max Lancing to his knees would be a pleasure.

At exactly ten minutes to the hour, Wilder leaned across to unlock the off-side door and a shabby young man with a drooping moustache slid into the back seat. He held out his hand, palm uppermost, and made impatient clicking noises with his tongue. When his fingers closed around the cool metal of the pistol, he sat back in his seat with a smile of childish delight on his face. It would not have surprised Wilder to discover that the prospect of owning a gun had held as much attraction for the man as had the offer of hard cash.

Joe Craven was in his mid-twenties. This was to be his first really important job. He had recently served a two-year prison sentence for petty theft and handling stolen property, a period which had brought him into close contact with the kind of hardened criminal he admired. The softly-spoken prison chaplain had dedicated long hours to teaching him to read, so opening his eyes to the stimulation of pulp magazines and helping to widen his ambitions in the world of crime. In his short lifetime of disorganized misdeeds, he had rarely managed to make an easy living, but this time, he was convinced, was going to be different. This time he was getting himself involved with professionals, men who knew what they were doing and how they were going to get away with it. He stood to collect enough cash from this job to take him to the big city in style. There was a whole new world out there for him to enjoy, and somewhere along the way, perhaps in some isolated farmhouse or week-end cabin, he might find out for himself what it felt like to cut a man's throat and watch him die.

It was three minutes to the hour when Wilder spotted Kevin Rey at the other end of the street. He was walking with his hands in his pockets and his jacket slotted through the crook of one arm. He stopped to examine the front window of Lancing and Warwick's before moving casually towards the car. He was a stocky man of medium height, whose features were so ordinary as to be instantly forgettable. Quiet and unemotional, he only made decisions after careful sifting of all the facts involved, then stuck to his plans through hell or high water. He was stubborn, unhurried, the kind of man who never acted on impulse. These qualities, coupled with the fact that he was not known to the police, made him a reliable second man to someone like Wilder.

Once inside the car, he took the offered pistol and placed it in the folds of his jacket. He did not share Craven's interest in weapons for their own sake. He saw them as tools, either for sport or for certain jobs, and as such, handled them with respect, nothing more.

'She's late,' he said, quietly. 'Do we wait?'

Wilder nodded his head briefly. 'That's the plan.'

'I can't see the point. Seems to me it would be better to move in as soon as Lancing's alone in the shop. Extra witnesses mean extra risks, and who needs a snivelling woman on the scene?'

'We wait,' Wilder said.

'You're the boss.' Rey's voice, like his face, was expressionless.

In the rear seat of the car, Joe Craven sat with his feet up on the upholstery and his nose buried in a back copy of *Crime Magazine*. Thrust inside his jacket, the fingers of his right hand still gripped the pistol.

Vince Wilder rubbed his eyes with his knuckles until tiny coloured lights flashed in the darkness behind the lids. He wriggled his left foot, trying to get rid of the tingling sensation which was spreading from his toes to his calves. A heat shimmer rose from the bonnet of the car, blurring his vision slightly. From the rear seat, a smell of sweat and stale tobacco reached his nostrils. The air inside the car was becoming decidedly unpleasant. It was too hot a day to be cooped up in a confined space with a man who obviously hadn't taken the trouble to wash.

'Shit this for entertainment,' he said through clenched teeth. 'I'm getting out to stretch my legs. You two stay in the car so we don't attract too much attention.'

He climbed from the car and slammed the door behind him, then stood on the pavement flexing his muscles and trying to kick the wrinkles from his trousers. He ran his thumbs behind his belt, letting in cool air to the band of perspiration which was sticking his shirt to his skin. His close-fitting gloves were causing his hands to sweat and adding to his discomfort, but he had no intention of removing them until the job was over. Even with no police record, he had no desire to leave his fingerprints behind for police files. Although Lancing and Warwick would hardly dare involve the police in the theft of an illegal diamond shipment, they would have to make an official complaint before an insurance claim could be made to cover the loss of the shop contents. Once the job was over, Vince Wilder needed to be certain that he could never be connected with it. He liked his business deals to be clean and efficient, with no loose ends. The guns and the extra man made his deal virtually riskless; the tight leather gloves were just one more detail of his careful planning.

He took out his comb and tidied his hair, using the window of a nearby dress shop as a mirror. Beyond the displays, a chubby salesgirl caught his eye and smiled. He winked at her and bowed slightly before returning to the car, where he stood with his forearms resting on the hard top. Briefly lowering his head, he sniffed the perfumed warmth of his own body, pleased by the faint but distinct aroma of wild herbs. A short sliver of wood protruded from his mouth. He moved it from side to side with his tongue, pushed it between his front teeth and chewed on it thoughtfully. In spite of the heat and the excitement of what he was about to do, he was perfectly relaxed.

Across the street, the last two members of Lancing's staff emerged from the shop, climbed into a waiting car and drove away. Seconds later, a cab drew up outside the shop and a young woman stepped out. She was slender but curvy, with well-shaped legs and a cascade of auburn hair which hung to her shoulders in soft curls and gleamed in the sunlight as she moved her head. The light-weight suit she was wearing accentuated her figure, its skirt swirling against shapely legs. She had the grace and confidence of a woman who took her beauty for granted. She tapped on the door of the shop and hesitated for a few seconds before going inside. Almost immediately, the blinds were rolled down over the door and the small side window.

Wilder got back in the car and started the engine, then drove slowly down the street to park in the spot vacated by the cab. He sat back in his seat, took a deep, slow breath and forced the air out through his nostrils.

'Right,' he said. 'Any questions?'

Joe Craven was sitting on the edge of his seat. His eyes were bright and he was grinning as he shook his head vigorously from side to side.

Kevin Rey glanced at his watch and took a long look up and down the street to make sure that their movements had gone unobserved. Then he took out the forged ID card and balanced it on the dashboard while he pulled on his jacket and eased the the pistol into a comfortable position. With only a brief nod in Wilder's direction, he left the car and walked towards the shop.

Vince Wilder crushed the matchstick between his teeth as Rey stepped back against the wall, trying to look as unobtrusive as possible as he kept his body clear of the door. Anticipation quickened his heart beat and over-heated his armpits. The planning and the waiting were over at last and the action about to start. He was smiling as he watched Rey approach the shop door with the folded card in his hand.

two

Max Lancing drew his mistress into his arms and kissed her warmly. There was a hint of peppermint on her breath, and her perfume was fresh and very light. They had not made love for more than a week, and the familiar softness of her body as she clung to him filled him with desire. He kissed her face and throat, nipped the lobe of her ear with his teeth and moved the palm of his hand across her body. Her response was instant. She pushed herself against him and lifted her face, her mouth seeking his. The warm tip of her tongue flicked across his lips. At the same time, her fingers slid down to the front of his trousers, stroking, caressing, filling him with a need that was urgent. He eased her towards one of the sofas and pushed her down on the cool leather upholstery, his fingers tugging at the buttons on her jacket. She stretched her arms above her head, licking her lips sensuously as the soft fabric fell back to reveal her naked breasts. She gasped as he kissed her, and her hands were trembling as she stroked the back of his head, guiding his mouth to the pink, erect nipples. She raised one knee so that her skirt slipped over her thighs to expose her flimsy white undies, and Lancing touched the moist warmth of her before fumbling with the zipper on his trousers.

'God, you excite me,' he murmured against her breast. 'I swear you're the most . . .'

They sprang apart as somebody rapped loudly on the shop door. An unseen hand turned the knob, rattled the door against the lock, then rapped again.

'Police. Open up.' The voice was deep and authoritative.

'For fuck's sake . . .' Lancing swore softly. He rebuttoned the waistband of his trousers and forced the zipper closed, wincing.

The rapping continued, growing louder.

Shirley Foster got up from the sofa and hastily fastened her jacket. She smoothed her skirt and took several slow, deep breaths as she tidied her hair with her fingers. There was a hot flush on her cheeks and a tell-tale brightness in her eyes. She blew her lover a kiss and smiled mischievously as he strode to the door. The bulge in his trousers was clearly visible, its shape well defined by the tightly stretched fabric. The untimely interruption would make him tense, and the tension in his body would heighten their enjoyment of each other.

Lancing lifted the dark green blind until he could see the man's face. He was in plain clothes, a broad, tired-looking man with nondescript features and short hair. He held up a partially folded ID card and looked bored.

A feeling of apprehension, which Lancing had learned to to accept as an occupational hazard, rose briefly at the prospect of an interview with an officer of the law, only to subside as he stared back at the man outside the door. He shrugged his shoulders and unlocked the door. As it started to open, the other man threw himself against it, flinging it back on its hinges with such force that Lancing lurched against a display counter. Instinctively, he tried to reach the alarm switch which was concealed behind the big desk at the other side of the room. A savage kick to his solar plexus stopped him in midstride and brought him to his knees. Shirley's scream of fear came to an abrupt end when the palm of a man's hand struck the side of her face with a blow that sent her reeling. She fell against Lancing and clung to him while he struggled to feed air into his lungs. By the time he had recovered sufficiently to raise his head, the violence was over and the intruders completely in charge. The door of the shop was bolted, its blind lowered. The heavier blinds of the main window were securely fastened, their close fit giving absolute privacy to those inside the shop.

Through a haze of pain, Lancing stared at each of the three armed men in turn. The man who had shown the ID card, and had brought Lancing to his knees with one skilled movement of his foot, was lifting items of jewellery from their display cases and stuffing them into a plastic refuse bag. He took what came to hand, regardless of quality or price. His face expressionless, he ignored the others as he cleared every shelf and display case of its contents.

A younger man with black hair and a large moustache was leaning against the desk with a pistol in his hand and an unpleasant leer on his face. He licked his lips as he eyed Shirley Foster in a way which most women would have found offensive. His zip-fronted jacket hung open to reveal a grubby T-shirt stretched across his chest so tightly that his nipples were visible. Slowly and deliberately, he scratched at the front of his trousers with his free hand.

The third man carried a sawn-off shotgun and looked as relaxed as a guest at a cocktail party. He stared back at Lancing with a smile which slowly stretched into a broad grin, creasing his eyes into dark slits and revealing large, strong teeth. The smile was friendly, but the gun made the situation deadly serious.

Lancing was thinking fast. Along with cash and other items of value, a shipment of illegal diamonds was locked in the vault below the shop, protected by a time-lock. Without the matching key, which was held by his partner, there was no way to bypass the lock until its cycle was completed at 8.30 a.m. on Monday. It was Saturday afternoon and his partner had already left for the week-end. Even if the gang knew of the existence of the basement vault, there was no way for them to get inside without that second key.

'You'll find more jewellery in the safe in the back room,' he said evenly. 'There's also about twelve thousand in cash. The keys are in my pocket.'

He pointed to the jacket which hung on the back of the chair behind his desk.

'Just take what you want and get out of here. We won't cause you any trouble.'

Without taking his eyes from Shirley Foster's face, the younger man reached over the desk and lifted the coat by its collar. He tossed it in Lancing's direction, then slid his body along the polished surface of the desk. As the movement brought him closer to her, Shirley Foster edged away until her lover's crouched body was between her and the gunman. She kept her eyes on Lancing, determined not to acknowledge the other man's interest in her.

'Get the keys and let's go.' The shotgun jerked slightly to add weight to its owner's words. The man's voice was calm, but threatening.

Lancing hauled himself to his feet. The kick to his solar plexus had taken him completely by surprise, giving him no opportunity to brace himself against its impact. It had bruised his muscles and winded him so badly that he still found it painful to take a deep breath. Once on his feet he managed, with some difficulty, to conceal his discomfort. Directed by the movements of the shotgun, he found his keys and started towards the back room.

Shirley gripped his arm. Though outwardly calm, her hand trembled. She was unwilling to be left alone in the shop with the other two men.

'Stay where you are, lady,' the man with the shotgun ordered.

She shook her head defiantly and moved closer to Lancing.

'I said, stay where you are,' the man repeated, and the smile on his face only served to strengthen the menacing tone of his voice.

Lancing held the fingers that had gripped his arm. He smiled steadily into the soft blue eyes.

'Take it easy,' he said quietly. 'This will only take a few minutes. When they've got what they came for, they'll leave us alone. Don't do anything silly. Don't give them any reason to harm us.'

She allowed Lancing to release her hand and walk away. Long after he had gone ahead of the gunman into the other room, she stared at the spot on the carpet where he had been standing.

Lancing could see Shirley from the corner of his eye as he stood in the back room just beyond the open doorway. He quickly opened the small safe and placed the entire contents on its top. There was a good deal of cash in small notes, half a dozen pieces of valuable jewellery, and several private documents. There was also a small box containing four uncut diamonds, each of which was worth a tidy sum to the right buyer.

The gunman pocketed the cash and valuables, then indicated the locked door leading to the basement.

'Open it,' he ordered.

'But there's nothing . . .'

'Don't argue, just open it.'

'But there's nothing down there,' Lancing insisted, struggling to keep his words and his manner casual. 'It's just an unused storeroom. It's full of dust and old boxes. There's nothing else down there.'

The man smiled back at him. He moved a matchstick in quick little jerks to one corner of his mouth, then brought it back again in the same way until it protruded between his front teeth. He was slightly shorter than Lancing, neither as broad nor as heavy, but there was a lightness about his body which indicated speed and strength. He looked to be in good shape, with not so much as an ounce of excess weight to slow him down. Proud as he was of his own well-proportioned body, Lancing would think carefully before taking on the younger man, even without the gun.

Still smiling, the man tilted his head towards the door.

'Open it,' he repeated, with just enough edge to his voice to let Lancing know that further argument would mean trouble.

Obediently, Lancing selected a key from his bunch and opened the door. He flicked on the single light and hesitated, not sure what his next move should be. It took him only a few seconds to remind himself that any move he did make would have to be determined by caution. This might simply be a check to make sure that there was nothing of value hidden in the basement. Prompted by a jab in the back with the shotgun, he went ahead of the gunman down the narrow stairs.

The small, windowless basement room was littered with old packing cases and dust-covered bits of furniture. Street noises filtered in through air vents which were at ceiling level, and the passing of heavy traffic caused a vibration almost like a shudder to run along one wall. It was a low, dimly-lit room, with a musty smell to indicate its lack of use. It in no way resembled a strong-room, yet concealed behind a stack of dirty cartons, its far wall housed what looked like a large bank vault.

The younger man kicked the cartons to one side and whistled through his teeth. Set into the huge iron door, the white-faced dial of the time-lock marked off the passing seconds with a soft and rhythmic tick.

'The key.' The gunman's free hand stretched out, demanding.

Lancing shook his head. 'You won't get it open,' he said, almost apologetically. 'It's protected by a time-lock, set to run until Monday morning. I have a key to the door itself, but I can't use it while the time-lock is set.'

'So, disconnect the damn thing.'

Lancing shook his head again. 'I can't do that. It takes two keys to bypass the timer, and I only hold one of them.'

The gunman scowled, his smile deserting his face for the first time since he had entered the premises. He backed up the stairs, keeping his gun aimed at Lancing, and called to one of the men in the upper room.

'Rey, get down here, fast.'

The light-haired man appeared almost immediately and padded down the stairs, his step surprisingly light for a man of his build. His grey eyes had the same bored expression as he glanced at Lancing before carefully examining the lock and the bunch of keys. His lips moved slightly as he calculated the hours remaining on the clock.

'Who has the other key?' he asked.

'My partner, George Warwick.'

'Where can we find him?'

Lancing shrugged his shoulders. 'He left around midday. Said he was going to pick up his daughter and take her to some show or other. He didn't say when he expected to get back. He likes to get away most week-ends.'

'Do you know where he lives?'

Lancing nodded.

'Does he live alone?'

'Yes, he's widowed.'

'No girl friend? No housekeeper?'

'Sometimes,' Lancing offered. 'Nothing permanent. A woman comes in to take care of the house, but I don't think anyone stays with him.'

The grey eyes scrutinized him for a long time, then, having apparently decided that he was telling the truth, the man turned away and stood looking at the heavy door.

'That's what we have, Wilder,' he said to his colleague without turning his head. 'I've seen one like this before. If you really want to get inside it, you'll have to wait till Monday morning or find that other key. Nothing short of gelignite will shift that door, and any interference will trigger the secondary alarm. What's in there, anyway?'

'Nothing for you to get interested in.'

'You mean, whatever it is, it's none of my business. Not part of the deal, huh?'

'That's right,' the man called Wilder agreed. He ground a matchstick between his teeth. Whatever was going on in his mind didn't show itself in his face.

The other man looked at Lancing, then back at Wilder. Without further comment, he padded back upstairs, his pistol held loosely at his side. Wilder jerked his head to indicate that Lancing should return to the upper room.

When they reached the shop, Shirley Foster moved quickly towards Lancing and leaned against him as he embraced her. He felt a shudder run through her slender body, and when he lifted her face he saw that her lipstick was smudged around her mouth. The top button had been torn from her jacket, leaving a small patch of broken threads in the fabric.

Lancing glowered at the young man who was standing by the desk. He stared back at Lancing with a leer, as if challenging him to raise an objection of some kind.

'You should teach your woman how to dress herself properly,' he sneered, when it was clear that Lancing intended to remain silent. 'If she was mine I wouldn't let her go around with her tits swinging loose. Gives a man ideas. Makes him hot in the crotch. Nice tits she's got, though . . . nice, fleshy tits.'

'Knock it off, Craven,' Wilder said coldly.

'Oh, come on, Vince. All I'm doing is complimenting the man on his woman . . .'

'I said, leave it alone. We have more important things to worry about than some woman's tits.'

'OK. OK. Anything you say, Vince, anything you say. Besides . . .'

He looked back at Lancing and grinned, then licked his lips slowly before adding:

'. . . I don't mind saving them . . . for later.'

Though Shirley stiffened in his arms, Lancing found it easy to ignore the taunt. He was watching Wilder, letting the name and the face blend together in his mind. He told himself that it didn't matter. It didn't even concern him if the police caught up with the gang after the robbery, or if they simply disappeared with their haul. His insurance would cover his legitimate losses, and now that Wilder had proof that the vault could not be opened, its uninsured, irreplaceable contents would remain intact. With that relief to modify his temper, he could afford to disregard the crudities of a leering young thug.

three

For several minutes, the man named Wilder stood to one side of the main door of the shop, squinting out through a gap in the blinds which he caused by lifting the stiffened fabric with his thumb. He was viewing the street through narrowed eyes, and the shaft of sunlight across his face revealed a fine layer of perspiration on his skin. His jaw moved continually as he ground his teeth against the remains of a matchstick. At last he snapped the blind back into place and spoke briefly to Rey, who nodded his head without comment.

Max Lancing and Shirley Foster were pushed to the back of the shop and made to stand with their heads against the wall and their hands clasped behind their backs. Using the barrel of his pistol, Rey nudged their feet back until the upper parts of their bodies were bent forward at an uncomfortable angle. Lancing gritted his teeth as his weight was pushed against the small area of scalp at the top of his head which was in contact with the wall. It was the position often forced on suspects by over-zealous police officers, and the indignity of it affected Lancing as much as did the strain on his muscles.

By his side, Shirley Foster's breathing was rapid and shallow. Her hair had fallen forward, hiding her face, but he knew that she must be under considerable stress. He suppressed a desire to offer her some kind of verbal encouragement. It did not seem likely that the gunmen would expect her to maintain such a position for more than a few minutes.

Across the room, Craven slouched on one of the sofas, his heavy shoes leaving marks on the soft leather. He was pointing his pistol at the prisoners, smiling as he watched Shirley Foster's body begin to tremble under the strain of her unnatural stance.

Kevin Rey was perched on one arm of the sofa with his weapon balanced across his knee. The plastic bag lay at his feet, bulging with pieces of jewellery and other valuable objects. Already the ornate crown of a silver figurine had torn a hole in the thin plastic.

In the back room Wilder, who was clearly the leader of the group, was using the telephone. He had closed the door behind him, and his voice was pitched low, so that his conversation could not be overheard. His behaviour implied that there might be a fourth member of the gang who needed to be consulted before a change of plan could be made.

With a whimper, Shirley Foster crumpled to the floor in a faint. Lancing dropped to his knees beside her, so relieved to have the pressure removed from his head that he didn't even pretend to go to her assistance. He watched the younger man, Joe Craven, swagger across the room with a satisfied smile on his face.

'Well, well, well,' the man drawled. 'And what have we here?'

'She's passed out,' Lancing said, wiping sweat from his brow with the back of his hand. 'You can't expect a woman to stand for long in that fashion . . . it's agony.' He touched the top of his head and winced at the tenderness of his scalp.

Craven pushed the hair back from Shirley's face with the toe of his boot, leaving a smudge of dirt across her damp cheek. He was still grinning when he looked back at Lancing.

'So, what's your problem?' he asked. 'Who gave you permission to move?'

'I was trying to help her . . .'

'Balls.'

'Look, I was just . . .'

'Get back against the wall, Lancing.'

'What the hell for? I'm in no position to make trouble. You can watch me just as well from here.'

The pistol was slowly raised until it pointed at the gap between Lancing's eyes. The finger on the trigger stiffened, and in spite of the cheerful expression on the gunman's face, the knuckles of the hand which held the gun were white.

'All right,' Lancing said quickly. 'All right.' He hauled himself to his feet and took up his previous stance with the top of his head pressed against the wall. The sharp kick to his shin from Craven's shoe was designed to shift his feet further from the wall, thereby increasing the pressure on his head. Instead it threw him completely off balance and he fell to his knees.

'Get up, Lancing.' The words were ground out between clenched teeth, and all humour had disappeared from his face.

Lancing got to his feet as quickly as he was able, but before he could fully regain his balance, another kick, this time to the back of his knee, sent him sprawling. The end of the pistol was rammed against the back of his neck with such force that he could not move his head.

'I said, get up.' The voice was close to his face, the breath hot and tobacco stained. 'On your feet, old man. You've one hell of a way to go before you can take a rest. Now get up, damn you.' He jabbed the pistol again into the tender flesh at the back of Lancing's neck, then stood back to allow him to get to his feet. He chuckled softly as his victim obeyed him.

'Hey, Kevin,' he called over his shoulder. 'Come over here and keep an eye on the shopkeeper while I take a closer look at his lady-friend.'

The other man crossed the room and leaned on the wall close to Lancing, who tensed as the barrel of the handgun touched his temple. In spite of the loaded guns, he had a sudden, strong temptation to lash out at the intruders. Only with much effort did he control his temper until the urge had passed.

'Don't give me any trouble,' Rey said quietly, as if reading his thoughts. 'This gun is fitted with a silencer, so I could blow your head apart without so much as disturbing a fly on the wallpaper.'

Lancing stood perfectly still. He could feel the blood pounding in his face, and part of his scalp felt as if it was being torn from his head. He knew that he must remain calm and unemotional. Any attempt at heroics would be foolhardy, especially when the only thing at stake was his own pride. He told himself that when the robbery was over, he would be thankful that he and Shirley were relatively unharmed. In order to make sure of that, all he had to do was keep his pride and his temper under control and do exactly as he was told.

Joe Craven was laughing as he thrust his gun inside his jacket and reached for Shirley Foster. He grabbed her by the hair and pulled her roughly to her feet, then held her against the wall with one hand while he slapped her face with the other. Her head jerked from side to side with the force of the blows, and when her eyes finally flickered open, he twisted her hair in his fingers to prevent her turning her face away from him. He pressed his mouth down on hers, chewing her lips with his teeth, pushing his tongue into her mouth and making crude animal noises. His hips gyrated against hers, pinning her to the wall, while with his free hand he yanked her skirt above her knees.

From his agonized position only a few feet away, Lancing could see the gunman's knees forcing Shirley's legs apart, and the grubby hand pulling at her skirt. He saw her body jerk in feeble protest and her hands try to lash out at her attacker. He wanted to yell at her to keep still, to warn her that her struggles would only excite the man further. Caution silenced him.

Craven pressed his body against Shirley's, stifling her cries with his mouth. Then, without taking his mouth from hers, he balled his right hand into a fist and struck her savagely in the stomach. When he released her, she uttered a long, choking cry and fell to the floor.

In spite of his efforts to maintain his self-control, Lancing was suddenly overcome by rage. With a roar of protest, he shoved himself away from the wall, fists clenched, face contorted with fury. He heard Craven laugh and reached for the man's throat, wanting to choke off the offensive sound. He could still hear the laughter when Rey's pistol came down across the back of his neck with a blow that knocked him senseless.

He was sprawled on the carpet behind the desk when he regained consciousness. Somebody had folded his jacket and pushed it beneath his head. His tie had been loosened and the top two buttons of his shirt were open. A throbbing pain in the back of his head reached down to his shoulders and across to his ears. When he tried to turn his head, a wave of nausea swept over him. Even the movements of his eyes caused him pain. He felt wretched.

'Lie still for a while. Don't try to move yet.' It was Wilder's voice. He sounded concerned.

Lancing tried to speak, but all he could manage was a loud groan. Perspiration tickled his skin as it gathered in his hairline and ran down his temples. He welcomed the coolness of the wet cloth which was placed on his forehead. When he opened his eyes again, Vince Wilder's face hovered above him, the dark eyes creased as he smiled. The handsome features were disturbingly familiar.

'How do you feel?'

'Lousy.' Lancing's voice was little more than a croak. He tried to push himself into a sitting position, but his efforts resulted in a stab of pain in his head and another wave of nausea. He fell back gasping, and lay still. Knowing that he had been struck with a heavy weapon by a powerfully-built man, he feared the damage which might have been done to his neck.

It was Shirley's face which he saw the next time he opened his eyes. She was dabbing gently at his face with the damp cloth. Her eyes were bright with unshed tears and she was very pale. He reached up and touched her face, stroking the bruised skin tenderly with his fingertips. One side of her mouth was swollen, and there were several small marks on her lips.

'They made me phone George,' she whispered. 'They were arguing about a key, and it made matters worse when I was unable to contact George. Who are these men, Max? What more do they want? Why can't they be satisfied with what they've already taken, and leave us alone?'

Lancing ignored her questions. 'Are you all right, Shirley?' he asked, instead.

'Yes,' she whispered, nodding her head and making a brave effort to sound cheerful. 'What about you?'

'I'll survive.'

'Does it hurt very much?'

Lancing stretched his lips into what he hoped was an acceptable substitute for a smile.

'Only when I laugh,' he said, and was disappointed by her lack of response.

'The one with the shotgun was furious when he saw what the others had done,' Shirley told him. 'He ordered them to keep their hands off us because . . .'

Her body tensed as a strong hand gripped her shoulder.

24

Without taking her eyes from her lover's face, she allowed Wilder to steer her to a corner of the room, where she sat down on the floor. Then she lowered her head until her face was hidden by her hair, relieved to be left alone in an inconspicuous place.

With Wilder's help, Lancing managed to sit up. The effort left him exhausted. His neck muscles felt as if they would collapse under the weight of his head, and he was unable to prevent himself moaning as Wilder's fingers massaged his neck and shoulders. The leather gloves were soft and supple against his skin, the hands firm, the movements practised. Within seconds, his pained muscles began to respond.

'He's a fool,' Wilder said. 'One of these days, he'll break a man's spine with that trick of his.' He continued the massage, his fingers kneading and squeezing the bruised flesh. After a long interval, he lowered his voice almost to a whisper and said:

'You and I are the only ones here who know what's in that vault, my friend. Let's keep it that way, shall we? As far as the others are concerned, you only keep private documents down there. Understand?'

Lancing nodded. He could feel Wilder's breath on his skin. The pain in his neck increased.

'Until I get what's in the vault,' Wilder continued, 'there's no way that you and your lady-friend are going to see the last of us. And if Rey or Craven find out what I'm after, you're a dead man, Maxie. It's that simple.' To add weight to his threat, he dug both his thumbs into the swollen, discoloured flesh, drawing an involuntary cry of pain from his victim.

Lancing slumped forward as the strong hands released him, and for a long time he could feel their pressure across his shoulders. He watched Wilder join his friends at the other side of the room near the main door. They had found some whisky in the back room and were taking turns at swigging it straight from the bottle. Wilder dipped into the plastic bag, found a small silver goblet and poured himself a drink. He arranged his body elegantly in a chair, smoothing the creases from his trousers before crossing his outstretched legs at the ankles and making himself comfortable. He sipped his whisky almost delicately from the long-stemmed goblet. He looked perfectly relaxed, but the eyes which watched Lancing through partly closed lids were wary, and the heavy shotgun across his knees was cocked, ready to fire.

Max Lancing rotated his head slowly in an effort to inject some strength back into his neck muscles. He breathed evenly as he flexed each shoulder in turn, forcing his body to ignore its pain. He kept a careful eye on the gang and tried to think calmly about his situation.

Lancing was wealthy, successful, and fiercely possessive of all that belonged to him. For many years he had schemed to get what he wanted, and everything he owned was a direct result of his own persistent efforts. The legitimate side of his business provided him with a fine house in a classy neighbourhood, with an impressive public life and the kind of social standing he and his wife had always wanted. The other side of his business fattened his Swiss bank accounts and sustained his private life, of which Shirley Foster was an important part. He could play the casinos without sweating, and he could afford to take big risks for big profits, knowing that all the security he needed was right there in the basement, behind the vault door. It was inconceivable that three thugs who had probably never done a real day's work in their lives, should walk in off the streets and snatch it all away from him. His insurance company would cover what was taken from this shop and the small safe, but the basement safe was another matter entirely. Apart from the illegal shipment of uncut stones, it contained over a quarter of a million in cash which had not, and could not be declared for tax purposes. It also contained a small but vital book listing enough names and details to put a half-dozen men behind bars and as many again out of business. Neither his Swiss accounts nor his numerous contacts would be of any use to him if he lost the contents of the vault. If the gang decided to hang around until Monday morning, or if George Warwick could be traced to provide the other key, Max Lancing was as good as finished.

For several minutes, Shirley Foster had been edging her way across the room. She knew that Wilder was watching her over the rim of his goblet, but his silence and lack of facial expression gave her the encouragement she needed to keep moving. She reached Lancing's side and snuggled close to him, welcoming the strong arm around her shoulders. He managed a smile of reassurance. She seemed small and fragile, far removed from the capable, independent young woman who had been his mistress for so long. He made up his mind there and then to take her to his week-end cabin just as soon as he could get things smoothed over after the raid. He was sure that a few quiet days in the open air would erase the unpleasantness that they were now having to endure. He sighed deeply and tightened his grip on her shoulder. Even in those circumstances, the closeness of her body excited him.

Lancing closed his eyes and tried to relax. He was counting on the gang giving up before the vault could be opened. Vince Wilder could only be guessing about the fortune sitting behind the time-lock. Somehow, he had found out about the second safe and his imagination was filling in the details. He had not known about the two keys needed to bypass the timer, which meant that he was unlikely to be working on inside information.

Lancing held Shirley in his arms and felt himself begin to relax. He was convinced that their ordeal would soon be over. The most important factor now, he felt, was that George Warwick should enjoy his week-end as far away from his house and the shop as possible. It shouldn't take long for a man like Vince Wilder to decide that a mere probability wasn't worth staking his freedom on. Already the gunman was checking his watch. All that was needed, as far as Lancing could see, was a cool head and a little more time.

four

It was almost midnight when Wilder shook Lancing awake and ordered him to ring George Warwick's number. Lancing was groggy and dry-mouthed. His head was throbbing and his arm stiff where Shirley had lain against it. That he had slept at all surprised him, that he had actually been asleep for around three hours was amazing, to say the least.

There was no reply from his partner's number. He smiled in the semi-darkness of the back room. He was looking forward to seeing the expression on old George's face when he explained to him just how close they had come to losing everything they had.

The shop was less dark than the small back room had been, with angular shafts of light streaming in from the street through the small gaps above the window blinds. Stretched out on the sofa, Joe Craven snored softly in his sleep. His fingers still circled the neck of the bottle he had been drinking from, which now contained no more than an inch of liquid.

Kevin Rey was sitting on the floor with his back against the wall and his head slightly bowed. He held his pistol in his left hand, its barrel balanced across his right forearm and his finger on the trigger. It was impossible to tell whether his eyes were closed or open. Just looking at him made Lancing feel nervous. One small jerk of his finger and he could blow someone's head off in his sleep.

At 1.30 a.m. Lancing dialled Warwick's number for the third time. There was still no answer.

'He won't come back tonight,' he whispered in the darkness.

'Shut up,' Wilder snapped.

They were standing in the back room, both tense and wary. The whole place was silent save for the rhythmic snoring in the next room.

'I tell you, he won't be back tonight. I know George pretty well. He never stays out this late if he intends coming back at all. Late nights don't agree with him. He's over sixty and over-weight. He can't take . . .'

The barrel of the shotgun touched the front of his shirt just above his belt. He could feel no movement in the heavy weapon, not even the slightest tremor. The hand which gripped it was perfectly still. When the pressure on his body increased, he edged back through the doorway and returned to his place beside the still sleeping Shirley. Without a word, Wilder cross-ed to the front window and leaned his shoulder against its frame, peering out at the street through a space at the edge of the blind. His profile stood out against the dim light, handsome and fine boned. He held his watch close to the window so that he could see the time, then jerked his head and spat a chewed matchstick into the room. He was growing restless.

Max Lancing could have leaned on the wall or curled up beside Shirley and slept. Instead, he sat cross-legged with his back straight and his head unsupported. The tender muscles of his neck and shoulders registered acute discomfort each time his head fell forward in sleep. Much as he needed more rest, an instinctive caution prompted him to remain awake and watchful. Unable to rely fully on his assumption that the gang would soon be gone, he wanted to keep the advantage they had over him to a minimum.

He watched Wilder walk silently into the back room, and heard the door to the lavatory open and close with a small click. He stared across to where Rey still sat with his back against the wall. He willed his eyes to penetrate the darkness, willed the gunman to give some small sign to indicate if he was awake or asleep. Caution warned him to ignore the opportunity which Wilder's absence offered, but his natural instincts were to take full advantage of any chance to tip the scales in his own favour. He wanted to end it right now, with no risk of Wilder getting his hands on the second key or coming back at some later date for another try at the vault.

Kevin Rey remained motionless while Lancing licked his lips and broke out in a cold sweat. All he needed was a few seconds to get across the room, and, the element of surprise would do the rest. He could grab Rey's pistol and shoot both men before either of them realized what was happening. Then he could go for Wilder. The darkness of the back room would give him the edge he needed, even against the shotgun.

Shirley Foster twitched in her sleep and started to whimper. Lancing was crouched, now, his eyes fixed on the shadowy shape at the other side of the room, and his body taut. He reached out and stroked Shirley's face. It was hot and damp. Her fingers grasped his hand and held it tightly, and she whispered his name as she tried to pull him closer.

Desperately, he yanked his hand free and began to propel his body forward. At the same time, the lavatory door opened and the back room was filled with the sound of running water. He was down on his knees before Wilder got through the door, holding Shirley in his arms and whispering comforting words against her hair. He was praying that Wilder had not seen enough to guess his intentions. He did not know whether to curse the woman in his arms or thank her. Her need for comfort might have robbed them of their only chance to beat the gang, but it might also have saved his life. Across the darkened shop, the man called Rey had not moved, but it would not have surprised Lancing to discover that he was watching them with a smile on his face.

His arm was cramped from supporting Shirley's weight for so long, and his fingers were tingling uncomfortably. He managed to ease himself free without disturbing her, once again surprised that he had fallen asleep so easily. It was too dark for him to see his watch, but he guessed that he had slept for at least an hour. The street outside was silent, completely free of traffic. Somewhere in the distance, the siren of a police car wailed in the night.

'And what the hell are we supposed to do when it gets light?'

Lancing recognized Rey's voice, even though the man spoke in a whisper. He lay where he was and listened.

'I say we move now,' Craven said in a louder voice. 'We're pushing our luck by hanging around here.'

Wilder was standing close to the window, his shotgun hanging in the crook of his arm. He seemed to be ignoring the other two men. He didn't even turn his head when Craven lurched to his feet and wagged a finger in his face.

'You're about to blow this job, Wilder,' he snorted. 'What in hell's name are we hanging around for, anyway? All right, so there wasn't much cash in the safe, but so what? There's enough to get us all away from here. All we have to do is drop the stuff with a fence, collect the pay-off, and get the hell away from this place.'

'He's right, you know,' Rey put in quietly. 'Whatever's in that vault can't be worth getting caught for. We've picked up what we came for, and it's enough for us to get started on, so let's move out while we still have the chance.'

Wilder took a fresh matchstick from his inside pocket and pushed it into his mouth. He chewed on it thoughtfully before clearing his throat and speaking in a low voice.

'It's not quite as simple as that,' he said. 'I've got my orders . . .'

'Orders?' Rey sounded surprised. 'What orders? I thought *you* were running this show?'

'That's what you were supposed to think.'

'That makes it a four-way split,' Craven cut in angrily. 'That makes it a sodding four-way split.' He was swaying slightly, due to the large amount of whisky he had consumed.

'All right. All right. There's no need to start getting worried about the split.'

'Like hell, there isn't . . .'

'Shut up, Craven,' Wilder barked. 'Shut up and listen to me. Everything we've picked up so far is for you and Rey. A two-way split, right down the middle.'

'Huh?' Craven sniffed noisily and wiped the back of his hand across his mouth. 'So where does that leave you? Where's your cut?'

'I get my pay-off directly from the boss when I hand him certain documents from that vault down there in the basement. This is a simple shop raid as far as you two are concerned, but for me it's a lot more. We stick together until the job's over, and there's no way we can walk out of here without those papers.'

31

There was a long silence, during which Lancing's blood ran cold. If Wilder was speaking the truth, then someone was after the book containing details of the diamond run. It listed names, dates, routes, and information about all his contracts. It was the only real insurance he had against being squeezed out of the dangerous games he played. It was like a time bomb. Its presence intimidated his enemies and kept his business associates in line, but all he had to do was make one little slip and it could explode in his face. If Wilder was really after the book, then someone big must be pulling the strings, someone on the inside who was big enough to organize the robbery, then use the information once he had it.

'So who's running things, Wilder?' Craven was slouching near the door. In the darkness his large moustache caused his profile to look like that of a Negro.

'Come on, now,' Wilder said with sarcasm. 'Surely you don't seriously expect me to tell you that?'

'And why the hell not? We're taking all the damn risks, so I reckon we have a right to know who it is we're taking them for.'

Rey was sitting on the arm of the sofa. He nodded his head in agreement, but said nothing.

'All right,' Wilder agreed, and the tone of his voice implied that he was smiling. 'I'm not at liberty to name names, so let's just say that this job is . . . er . . . syndicate connected.'

'Christ Almighty!' Rey said, through clenched teeth. The simple oath was weighted with anger.

Craven whistled softly. 'Hey, that means we're in line for a pat on the back and a chance at some really big jobs if we pull this one off. It means we've hit the big time. The only way we go from here is *up*.' He sounded delighted, like a child who had suddenly discovered that he was to be allowed to play with the big boys.

'It means,' Rey answered bitterly, 'that we're in for a bullet in the head if we don't give them what they want. You're a bastard, Wilder. You didn't mention syndicate connections when you brought us in on this deal.'

'What the hell, Kevin, don't you like the idea of moving into the big league?'

'Don't give me that shit. I don't like the idea of being a marked man. If we don't make it, we're as good as dead, and if we *do* make it, we're put on the Big List so they can call us in any time they want a job doing in our area. I'm a free agent, Wilder, and I prefer to keep it that way.'

Wilder shrugged his shoulders. 'I don't think you have any choice, Kevin. The boss needs those papers, and there's no way we can get out of making the delivery. Don't worry, this might be a one-off, as far as you're concerned. There's no guarantee that you'll be called in on another job.'

Rey snorted and got to his feet. He stood looking at Wilder for a while, then walked angrily into the back room, slamming the door behind him.

Lancing lay in the darkness with his mind racing. It had to be a bluff. Wilder had to be lying to keep the other two in line. This didn't have the feel of a syndicate operation. It was too bitty. Wilder had all the hallmarks of the professional criminal, but he didn't know enough about this particular job to be working with heavy backing. Whoever was pulling the strings in the background had made an educated guess that the safe was worth robbing. He didn't believe that it was any more organized than that, whatever Wilder chose to tell his men.

Craven gulped the last of the whisky and dropped the empty bottle over the back of the sofa. He lit a cigarette, cupping the lighted match in both hands so that his features were briefly illuminated. He drew smoke deep into his lungs and held his breath before forcing it out again through clenched teeth. Slouched comfortably on the sofa, he seemed unconcerned at the prospect of a long wait before the job could be completed, but there was no way to assess how long it might take before his temper, like Rey's, started to fray.

Lancing lay with his eyes closed and lips slightly parted, taking slow, steady breaths and trying to clear his mind of unanswered questions. He had no intention of allowing himself to waste valuable mental energy on premature and perhaps unfounded worries. A man could die of fright without ever coming face to face with real danger, if he didn't keep a check on his imagination. It would be too easy for him to litter his mind with a hundred probabilities which caused so much sweat and confusion that he would be in no condition to deal with what was actually happening to him. Wilder was calling the tune. All Lancing could do was hang back and make sure that he was ready with the right steps when the time came for him to dance.

As he relaxed almost into a doze, he was aware of every sound in the room. He heard Rey pad softly from the back room and allow his heavy body to flop down on the arm of the sofa. His ears picked up the sounds as Craven bit off tiny slivers of finger nail and spat them out, making soft popping noises with his tongue. He was even aware of the faint noise Wilder made as he snapped the end off a fresh matchstick before putting it into his mouth. Weary but alert in the darkness, he heard footsteps on the carpet and stiffened. The toe of a shoe nudged his shoulder.

'Get up, Lancing.'

He followed Wilder into the next room, where he was permitted to use the lavatory before dialling George Warwick's number.

'He has an extension phone right beside his bed,' he said, when the number had been ringing for some time. 'He would have heard it by now.'

Wilder cursed under his breath. 'All right, Lancing. Get back in there with the girl. It looks like we'll have to make a slight adjustment to our plans.'

Lancing fumbled in the darkness until his hands found Shirley's body, then quickly stepped over her and sat down close to the big desk. Wilder seemed not to notice his changed position, and he breathed a sigh of relief when the gunman returned to the window and resumed his position of watchfulness.

Behind the desk, set neatly into the wall about one metre from the floor, was the small, white button which activated the shop alarm bell. If he could press that button, Wilder would be forced to abandon his plan to rob the vault, so his precious book, his diamonds, and his clients' cash would be safe. If he could inch his way round the desk without being seen, and get his finger on that vital button, it would all be over. The gang would run like three frightened rabbits.

He had edged his way to within a yard of the wall when he began to take into consideration the possible results of his actions. Startled by the alarm, the gunmen were likely to open fire on their captives before making good their escape. Craven and Rey had already shown how little they cared whether the prisoners lived or died. To activate the screaming, persistent alarm might prove to be no less deadly than pulling the trigger of a gun aimed at his own head. Tight-lipped with frustration, he eased himself back to where Shirley lay. He was unable to make a move without putting their lives in danger. Though it galled him to assume such a submissive role, he knew that he must continue to squat on the floor like a caged animal until a more suitable opportunity to retaliate presented itself.

From the other side of the room, the sound of running water hitting the carpet caught his attention. Joe Craven was leaning on the back of the sofa with his legs wide apart, urinating, He aimed the jet into a corner some distance away, and the splashing sound increased as the carpet became saturated.

'There's a lavatory in the back room,' Wilder said contemptuously.

Craven zipped up his trousers and adjusted his belt. 'Sure, boss,' he drawled.

'Use it,' Wilder snapped. 'Only animals piss on the floor.'

'Oh, come on. Who the hell cares, anyway?'

'*I* care, Craven.'

Lancing watched the dark shapes of the two men as they faced each other, but the flare-up he was expecting never came. Instead, Craven sat down on one arm of the sofa, his fists pushed deep into his jacket pockets. As Wilder resumed his vigil at the window, his rigid stance betrayed something of the irritation he was feeling.

five

Shirley Foster stirred restlessly in her sleep. Perspiration had dampened her face, plastering her hair across her cheeks and forehead in untidy tendrils. She hugged her stomach, drawing up her legs as if trying to ease some distressing pain. She was moaning softly.

'Hush, Shirley . . . everything's all right,' Lancing whispered. 'Hush, go back to sleep.'

He reached over to pat her thigh in a gesture of reassurance, but at the touch of his hand, she jerked away from him and awoke with a startled cry.

'It's all right,' Lancing hissed. 'Be quiet . . . it's me . . . it's Max.' He spoke softly but firmly, gripping her wrist at the same time and shaking it sharply. He wanted to calm her down before she could attract the attention of the gang.

When she realized who had touched her, a sob of relief caught in Shirley's throat. She pushed herself closer to him, grabbing at his shirt and pushing her face against his chest. She was weeping quietly, and he didn't blame her for her tears. Waking to find the nightmare still in progress must have come as a shock to her, and the fact that she was in pain from Craven's blow would greatly increase her distress. He tried to soothe her with whispered words, but her sobs grew louder with each breath she took. He stroked her face and held her as tightly as he could without hurting her. He could feel her heart racing and her fingernails biting into his flesh as she clung to him. He pushed her face against his shirt front and held it there. He could feel her teeth through his shirt and her tears soon penetrated the light fabric to make a warm, damp patch on his chest hair. Hysteria was building up in her.

'Shut up,' he hissed against her ear. 'For God's sake, keep quiet, you stupid bitch.'

His deliberately cruel words shocked her into silence, but for no more than a few seconds. She stiffened in his arms, her body almost rigid and her sharp fingernails gripping like talons in the flesh of his back. Then she took a deep, shuddering breath, lifted her face away from his body, and screamed.

Lancing clamped a hand over her mouth and gripped as hard as he could. His fingers crushed her already bruised lips, but he held on, gritting his teeth to add strength to his grip.

In response to the sudden noise, Joe Craven leaped to his feet and almost hurled himself across the room.

'What in fuck's name does she think she's playing at?' he snarled, dropping into a crouch beside the struggling woman. Behind him, Rey observed the scene without comment, his pistol held at waist level and pointing towards the shadowy figures.

'She's scared,' Lancing gasped.

'Shut her up.'

'You hurt her ... that punch in the stomach ...'

'For fuck's sake, shut her up.'

'I'm trying to ...' Lancing was holding her shoulders with one hand as he stifled her screams with the other. She fought him, clawing at his face and trying to bite his fingers.

'Shut her up,' Craven repeated, his tone menacing.

Lancing was having to employ all his strength to control the struggling Shirley and prevent her screaming out loud. His efforts brought fresh spasms of pain and weakness to his shoulder and neck muscles. The pressure of his hand stifled her cries to choking sounds which became trapped in her throat, but he did not know how long he could hold her in that manner. He was tempted to yell at her and slap her into silence, but before he could gather his senses sufficiently to act, Rey's pistol nudged the back of his neck and Craven shoved him roughly aside. Before Shirley could suck in enough breath for another scream, Craven lifted her by the hair and delivered a cruel slap to her face. Then he gripped her by the throat and spat angry words into her face.

'Shut your mouth. Shut your fucking mouth before I choke you.'

He tossed her aside as if she weighed nothing, and she fell to the floor, trembling in fear. As the gunmen moved away, Lancing pulled her into his arms and rocked her gently. Anger and humiliation caused a tightness in his throat which no amount of swallowing would remove. It shamed him to stand by helplessly while a thug like Craven manhandled his mistress.

Vince Wilder emerged from the back room at the same time as heavy footsteps sounded on the pavement outside the shop. He dropped silently into the shadows behind a display stand. At the other end of the room, his companions crouched in the darkness.

The footsteps halted close to the side window, and the broad back of their owner was faintly outlined against the blind.

'This shotgun is pointing right at your belly,' Lancing was warned. 'If you try anything heroic, you and the woman are as good as dead.' Wilder's voice was low and unhurried. He sounded almost casual.

Joe Craven scuttled across the carpet in a swift crawl. He nudged Lancing's arm with something hard and sharp.

'Any more noise out of your tart, and I'll slit her throat.'

The knife pressed against Lancing's cheek. Its blade was cool, its edge razor-sharp on his skin. He didn't doubt for one second that Craven would carry out his threat. He gave Shirley's hand a firm squeeze, hoping that she understood the danger they were facing. Another outburst of hysteria from her might kill them both.

Nothing happened for several tense and silent minutes. It was not possible to tell if the person outside was making any attempt to look into the shop. Only a wide, dark shape was visible beyond the blind, a shape which was a threat by its very presence.

Lancing's breathing was shallow and his ears strained for every sound. He tried to keep his mind clear so that he would be able to take advantage of any opportunity which might present itself. Refusing to dwell on guesses or probabilities, he knew only that somebody was standing outside the shop. As long as that person remained there, Lancing's own position was critical.

The footsteps started up again and moved to the front of

the building. A match scraped several times against the door frame, then the man outside started to cough as if the smoke from his cigarette had choked off his air supply. When his coughing fit subsided, he cleared his throat and spat into the street. This short series of unpleasant noises was completed by a string of profanities.

Craven sniggered in the darkness. He repeated a particular obscenity, giving it the same slurred emphasis. 'That's a new one on me,' he whispered, and continued to repeat it, between sniggers, long after the man outside had fallen silent.

'Shut up,' Rey hissed, waving his hand impatiently in Craven's direction. He crawled a little closer to the door and rested his ear against the wooden frame just a few inches from the floor. He drew back only slightly as the door rattled under the strain of a heavy body slumping against it. Seconds later, he crawled back across the room and spoke quietly to Wilder.

'Some old drunk with a skinful. Stinks of booze and piss, and by the sound of it, he's passed out with his back against the door. What do we do now?'

Wilder sucked air through his teeth, then made a whistling noise as he blew it out in the same way.

'I spoke to the boss just a few minutes ago,' he said. 'We're moving out.'

'Out?' Rey paused. He had been about to say something, but on second thoughts had decided against it. He deliberately confined his comments to the immediate problem.

'It's not going to be easy with that slob sleeping it off out there.'

'No problem,' Craven cut in cheerfully. He held up his knife so that the blade gleamed in the dim light. 'I can take care of him in three seconds. Just say the word, and he'll be dead before . . .'

'Don't talk such fucking shit.' Rey's voice was so unexpectedly loud that Shirley winced and put her hand to her mouth in alarm. She had almost cried out again. Lancing took her firmly by the arm, at the same time shifting his crouched position so that his weight was on his knees. He was prepared to shove her out of the way if trouble started.

Rey's left hand shot out and grabbed Craven by the front of his grimy T-shirt. He yanked him closer, ignoring the big knife which was close to the side of his face.

'Now you listen to me, Crud, and get this right first time,' he snarled. 'We didn't come here to kill some poor drunken bastard who happened to pass out in the wrong doorway. We didn't come here to kill *anyone*.'

'It was just an idea . . . an idea,' Craven protested. He glanced hopefully at Wilder, but his attention was jerked back to Rey as the grip on his shirt tightened.

'You were hired as a back-up man, Craven, not a damn assassin. Got that?'

Craven nodded vigorously. More prudent than scared, he accepted Rey's rebuke. When Rey released him, he fell back on his heels and remained there with his shoulders hunched. The blade of his knife rested against Lancing's outstretched hand. He pressed on it, feeling the knuckles move under the flat metal.

'Go sit over by the door and keep an eye on the drunk,' Wilder said to Craven. 'If he makes a move, let me know.'

'You're the boss.' Craven's reply was amiable. He smiled at Wilder, then turned his face slightly so that he could look at Lancing. His smile did not falter, nor did he look away from Lancing as he got to his feet. With a discreet twist of his wrist, he tilted the blade on to its edge and sliced it across the back of the outstretched hand before moving away.

Lancing gasped. He jerked his hand away and covered the wound with his other palm, feeling the warm blood on his skin.

'What's the matter?' Wilder asked.

'Nothing.' Lancing lied instinctively. If he told the truth, Craven would certainly make sure that he regretted it. The incident had illustrated a kind of pecking order whereby Craven, unable to improve his 'Third man' status in the gang, could gain perverse satisfaction by lashing out at Lancing. In order to protect himself, Lancing would, in effect, be forced to protect Craven.

'Nothing,' he repeated, reluctantly accepting the role Craven had created for him. 'Nothing at all.'

'Did you mean what you said about getting out of here?' Rey asked. Instead of looking at Wilder as he spoke, he was watching Lancing and Shirley, who had made themselves comfortable with their backs against the side of the desk. The girl looked as if she might be asleep.

'That's right,' Wilder confirmed.

'But what about the vault? What about those important documents your boss is supposed to want so badly?'

'Do I detect a note of mistrust, Kevin?'

'Do I get an answer to my question?' Rey countered.

Wilder smiled and tugged at the cuffs of his gloves, flexing the fingers of both hands in turn.

'We'll move out just as soon as we can, and hole up some-where safe until we can get hold of that other key. There's no problem. Nobody's likely to miss the lovebirds until Monday, by which time we should be gone with everything we need.'

'And if we don't contact this guy Warwick?'

'We'll just have to hit the vault on Monday morning when the time-lock is released.'

There was a long pause before Rey asked: 'Have you worked out how to stop Lancing raising the alarm two minutes after we're gone, if we have to do the job on Monday? Even if we tie him up and gag him, as planned, the alarm will be raised by the first damn customer who can't get into the shop.'

'Don't worry,' Wilder said. 'He and the girl won't be around to cause any trouble. They'll be under lock and key in a safe place until we're well away. All it'll take is a quick telephone call to put them back in circulation, and before then, the police won't have anything to go on, will they? I'm not about to blow this job, Kevin. No matter how long it takes, or how complicated it gets, I intend to see this through to the bitter end and come out laughing.'

'Jesus fucking Christ . . . it's the cops!' Craven suddenly yelled in a hoarse voice.

Lancing snapped his eyes open and placed his palm over Shirley's mouth. The skin across his knuckles was tight and painful where Craven had slashed him. He felt the wound open at one end and start to bleed again as he moved his fingers.

Wilder edged closer, resting the shotgun on his raised knee and aiming it at Lancing's chest. Rey was pressed up against the wall, squinting out through the edge of the blind. When the slow-moving patrol car came to a halt outside the shop, he lowered the blind and drew back, away from the window. Both car doors opened, then slammed shut. Heavy boots sounded on the pavement outside, stopping just beyond the door, less than a man's stride away from Craven's head.

'Hey, come on. You can't sleep here.' The voice was firm and even, designed to indicate authority without provoking a hostile reaction.

'Come on, old man. Let's get you out of here.'

There were the sounds of a struggle and muttered curses as the drunk was bundled into the car. After several minutes of waiting for the engine to start and the patrol car to move away, Wilder hissed at Rey through clenched teeth.

'What the hell's going on?'

'They're just sitting there,' Rey called back. 'Smoking, talking . . . hold on a minute . . . one of them's getting out . . . hell, he's coming back this way.'

Rey dropped the blind back into place and edged his way into the corner, where the shadows were deepest. Near the door, Joe Craven flattened his body to the carpet and remained perfectly still.

A strong hand tested the door against its lock. It barely rattled, due to the strong inside bolts which the gunmen had fastened when they first entered the shop.

'Best check the windows, Sam,' the man in the car called out. 'Just to be on the safe side.'

His partner obeyed, pressing his face to the glass and trying to peer past the dark shades. Against the small side window, his outline was clearly defined.

'Nothing to see,' he said at last. 'Looks all right to me.'

'OK, Sam, get in and let's get our friend here tucked up for the night.'

After a short time, the engine purred into life and the patrol car moved smoothly away. At the end of the street it waited, perhaps while the occupants scanned the darkened buildings for any sign of intrusion, then it turned left, picking up speed as it headed south along Buckham Road.

Max Lancing let the air out of his lungs in a long sigh. He felt Shirley relax against him, her body limp as the tension of the last few minutes drained from her. Lancing was grateful that the threat of panic and possible gunfire was over, yet even as he acknowledged his relief, he felt a vague disappointment. While the two police officers had been so close, he had crouched in the darkness facing Wilder's shot gun, and willed them to go away. Now that they were no longer out there, he regretted his own inaction, and wondered if the risks involved in attracting their attention might not have been worthwhile. A few moments before, silence and inaction had seemed logical, the only possible alternative to being shot dead by desperate men. Now that the danger had passed, he was left with a sense of shame. His instincts had been in control, but his conscience now told him that he had made a grave mistake. He should have done something.

Kevin Rey crossed to the other side of the window and lifted the blind so that he could watch the patrol car until it was out of sight. He surveyed the street for a full two minutes before lowering his pistol and moving back into the centre of the room.

'All clear,' he said, and there was no trace of fear or even tension in his voice.

Joe Craven whistled and slapped his palm on his knee. He was laughing as he got to his feet. The excitement of coming so close to being apprehended in the act of armed robbery seemed to appeal to him.

'Right,' Wilder announced, getting to his feet and shaking the creases from his trousers. 'Let's get the hell out of here.'

six

Lancing was ordered to put on his jacket before his hands were tied behind his back with his own necktie. He winced as the tough silk bit into his wrists. Joe Craven grinned as he ran his fingers over his handiwork.

'That tight enough for you, Lancing?' He prodded the taut flesh which bulged over Lancing's bonds. Apart from the simple act of securing his prisoner, he clearly felt that he still had a point to make. Before tying the final knot, he jerked both ends of the necktie so that Lancing emitted a small but distinct cry of pain.

When Craven bound Shirley Foster's wrists with a length of cord cut from one of the window blinds, she began to whimper. Instead of easing the pressure on her wrists, he took out his handkerchief and tied it tightly round her mouth. When he shoved her towards the door, she tripped and fell headlong.

'That's enough, Craven.' Wilder crossed to where Shirley lay and bent over her. For a moment their shadows became one in the darkness.

'It's much too tight,' he said at last. 'What're you trying to do, Craven, give her gangrene?'

'You told me to tie her wrists.'

'Sure I did, but that doesn't mean you have to torture her.'

'I was only following orders, Mr Wilder, sir.'

Wilder slowly got to his feet. Even in the dim light, it was easy to see that he was taller and more powerfully built than Craven. He spat the sliver of wood from the corner of his mouth without turning his head.

'Slacken the cord,' he said. 'No arguments, no back-talk, just slacken the cord.' He walked back to where Lancing was standing and examined his wrists.

'And then you can come over here and slacken these,' he added.

'You're the boss.' Although it was said lightly, there was a hint of sarcasm in Craven's tone.

'Where's your car?' Wilder asked Lancing.

'Round the back of the shop. In the yard.'

'Keys?'

'Here in my pocket. Left-hand side.'

Wilder found the keys and handed them to Rey.

'You know which is Lancing's car, Kevin. Bring it round to the front of the shop, and make sure you're not seen. Don't use the lights unless you have to.'

Light streamed into the shop from the street when Rey opened the door. He checked the street in both directions before ducking round to the rear of the building. In the few seconds before the door closed behind him, the empty shelves and display cases were illuminated, revealing an unfamiliar starkness. Lancing caught a glimpse of Shirley and was shocked by what he saw. The gag cut cruelly into her face, forcing her mouth open and dragging the skin across her cheeks so tightly that her face was robbed of its beauty. He wondered, guiltily, how much of the bruising around her mouth had been caused by his efforts to stop her screaming during her fit of hysteria. He was glad when the door closed, shutting out the light and hiding her face once more in shadow.

'I could take her, you know, Lancing. I could take your woman away from you and hold her until you produce that key.' Wilder spoke softly. He ran his fingers over Lancing's hands and wrists, making sure that the necktie had been loosened sufficiently. The movements of the gloved hand were as gentle as a caress on Lancing's skin.

'Think about it,' Wilder continued. 'Even if I swore on a stack of bibles that she'd come to no harm, you wouldn't really be sure. You couldn't know for certain that you'd get her back, intact, once you'd kept your side of the bargain.'

Lancing made no comment. He watched Craven hoist Shirley to her feet and glance at Wilder before stepping away from her. She was left standing in the centre of the room with her head bowed. She was close enough to hear Wilder's words.

'Is she worth it, Lancing? Is your lady-friend worth whatever it is you keep in that vault of yours?'

'Of course she is,' Lancing snapped, and realized immediately that his answer had been a little too fast and too loud to be fully convincing.

'That sounds like a good idea, boss.' Craven's voice came from the shadows near the door, where he was leaning with his back against the wall. 'Let's take the woman hostage. That way, we make sure the shopkeeper comes across with the key, and the waiting doesn't get to be a drag . . . not with pretty little Shirley to keep us company.'

Lancing narrowed his eyes and scowled at the shadows which hid Shirley's face. He knew that she had raised her head and was watching him, but it was too dark for him to see her clearly.

'Do you reckon he'd pay the ransom?' Wilder asked. He sounded amused.

'Sure he would, boss. No man'd turn his lady over to a bunch of unsavoury characters like us, without making some kind of a deal to get her back.'

'But would he keep his side of the deal, or would he sacrifice the girl for the goodies?' Wilder made soft, clicking noises with his tongue. He seemed to be thinking aloud, weighing up the pros and cons of his own suggestion.

'Well, Lancing, what d'you say? If we make some kind of deal, with the girl as hostage, will you stick to your side of it?'

'I'm willing to listen,' Lancing said cautiously.

'You mean, you're ready to negotiate?'

'Put it any way you like, Wilder. What did you have in mind?'

The gunman was silent for a moment, then his voice was sharply decisive when he said, 'Simple. We take the girl, and you buy her back.'

'How much?'

'Everything in that basement fortress of yours . . . *everything.*'

Lancing licked his lips. This was the hard part, convincing Wilder that a deal was possible. The rest, in spite of the potential danger to Shirley, would be relatively easy.

'You have a deal,' he said. 'I'll do whatever you say.'

Wilder moved forward until he was standing right in front

of Lancing. Shadows heightened his cheekbones and deepened the hollows of his cheeks, giving him a gaunt appearance. His breath was light on Lancing's face, with a faint antiseptic smell, as if he had recently used a mouthwash. He smiled, stretching his lips very slowly over his teeth. Lancing returned the smile, feeling that they were in agreement.

'Liar!' Wilder suddenly hissed.

'What the hell . . . ?'

'Liar!' Wilder repeated, louder now, and with something like anger in his voice. The smile had vanished from his face, and he stared back at Lancing through cold, narrowed eyes.

'I've seen you from every angle, Lancing,' he said. 'I know how you work, think, and figure the odds on everything you get involved with. Given just half the chance, you'll stash your pile and leave the girl to take her own chances. I reckon you might even bring in the police, just to cover yourself and satisfy your conscience.'

'You're wrong,' Lancing said, evenly. 'I'd keep my word. She's worth it.'

'Balls!' Wilder exclaimed, smiling again. He tapped his forefinger against the hairy patch which showed itself above the buttons on the other man's shirt. His voice had regained its warmth and its hint of amusement. 'You know . . . and I know . . .' he said slowly, '. . . . that *no* woman is worth that much.'

Lancing returned Wilder's stare, dismayed that his own thoughts had been so accurately voiced.

'Go in there and try Warwick's number again,' Wilder ordered. He waved his shotgun in the direction of the back room.

Lancing hesitated, looking over to where Craven leaned, barely visible against the dark wall. He was reluctant to leave Shirley alone in the shop with the most obnoxious member of the gang. Wilder noted the pause and nodded his head, smiling.

'Point taken,' he said quietly, then reached out and took Shirley by the arm, steering her towards the back room. He left her outside the door, where she was out of Craven's reach and could be seen by Lancing as he used the telephone.

Across the room, Craven cleared his throat with a grunting sound and spat on the carpet. Then he began to whistle, quietly and tunelessly. Lancing's self-satisfaction was two-fold. In protecting Shirley from his advances, he felt that he had scored against the gunman.

Predictably, there was still no reply from Warwick's number. He was not the kind of man who allowed his leisure hours to slip by unused, and he seldom spent long periods at his home. He would probably stay the night at his daughter's flat in town, as he had done many times before, in order to make an early start on their Sunday morning outing.

Wilder cleared the line and dialled again, carefully selecting each digit by fingering the dial. The receiver was wedged against Lancing's ear and held in place by his bruised shoulder. The strain of keeping it there was agony for his stiffened neck muscles. After what seemed like an age of listening to the persistent ringing tone, he was relieved when Wilder lifted the receiver to his own ear and cursed softly before dropping it back on to its cradle.

'Where the hell is he?' he demanded irritably.

Lancing shrugged his shoulders, then, realizing that his gesture would go unseen in the darkened room, said, 'I don't know. We don't keep tabs on each other's movements. I've never needed to contact him outside business hours.'

'You need to right now,' Wilder reminded him.

In response to a nudge with the shotgun, Lancing started to leave the back room. As he re-entered the shop, he almost collided with Joe Craven, who was leaning on the door frame with his pistol hanging loosely at his side. He had crossed the room silently, and Lancing wondered if his stealth had been designed to allow him to eavesdrop on the telephone call, or to bring him closer to Shirley. He was tempted to kick out at the leg which protruded across his path. A feigned stumble would give him an opportunity to bruise the gunman's shins, a prospect which was difficult to resist. Ignoring the grinning face so close to his own, and awarding himself a mental pat on the back for self-control, he stepped over the extended leg and stood close to Shirley.

Kevin Rey re-entered the shop with barely a sound. He closed the door behind him and handed back the car keys.

'So, what's the plan, Vince?' he asked.

'I want you and Craven to take the hired car and follow me. I'll take Lancing's car and the girl.'

Shirley stiffened and pressed herself close to Lancing.

'And Lancing?' There was something like mistrust in Rey's voice.

'He'll be with you and Craven.'

'And the stuff? What about that?'

'I'm carrying the cash and you're carrying the goods. What's your problem, Rey?'

'No problem,' Rey shrugged. 'I just like to know the score, that's all. What about the door?'

'I'll see to it. I've got the keys right here. All you need to worry about is keeping me in sight when we drive. Don't do anything that might attract attention. I need Lancing to get inside that vault, and we don't want the cops messing things up for us now we've come this far. I'm counting on you to keep everything running smoothly.'

He leaned forward and rubbed his nose deliberately so that his last words were muffled against his glove. 'Keep an eye on Craven. He could foul us up without even trying.'

Standing close to the two men, Lancing was able to hear everything that was said. He admired the way Wilder dealt so casually with Rey. It was exactly how he himself would have handled the situation. The instant a subordinate expresses so much as a hint of a doubt, pat him on the back, pretend to take him into your confidence, and convince him that his services are invaluable. If his personal status can be further inflated by favourable comparisons with an inferior, so much the better. By setting up Rey as watchdog over Craven, Wilder had increased the likelihood of cooperation from both men, and he had managed it with a minimum of words and effort. Obviously satisfied by the brief exchange, Rey grasped the bag containing the stolen valuables and crossed to the door.

At a signal from Wilder, Lancing was bundled into the front passenger seat of the gang's car. After a short, whispered argument, Rey slid into the back seat while Craven settled himself behind the wheel. Lancing craned his neck to watch Wilder lock the shop door and lead Shirley towards the pale blue Porsche which was parked right outside the door. Within seconds, the Porsche was pulling away from the kerb and heading for the far end of the street.

Craven cursed under his breath as he slammed the car into gear and swung out after Wilder. His breath filled the car with the smell of whisky, in spite of the fact that the window next to him was wound right down.

Lancing stiffened in his seat. The man wasn't fit to drive. He swung the car too sharply into each bend, and on two occasions mounted the pavement dangerously close to traffic signs. He aimed the car at a stray cat, swore obscenely when he missed it, and swung back into lane after narrowly missing a fire hydrant. At the next set of traffic signals, the Porsche came to a halt and Wilder got out. He strode to the second car and yanked open the door on the driver's side.

'Get out, you stupid crud,' he ordered. 'Rey, you should know better than to let him drive with all that whisky inside him. What are you trying to do, invite every cop in town to stop us on a trivial traffic offence? Come on, Craven. Out!'

Craven was gripping the wheel with both hands and staring at the road ahead. His lips were pulled into a tight line, adding emphasis to the steady pulse which throbbed in his cheek.

'I said, *out*,' Wilder repeated.

Leaning over from the rear seat, Rey jabbed Craven in the back of his neck with his pistol, a gesture which prompted the younger man into action.

As the gunmen changed places, Lancing stared at the back window of his Porsche. Shirley's face was just visible over the back of the seat, her features almost hidden by her tangled hair and the tight gag. She was healthy and agile, and surely not important to Wilder and his men. Even with her hands tied behind her back, it should be possible for her to get out of the car and run. It was unlikely that any of the gang would shoot her down in the open, and her escape would force them to abandon the rest of their plans and flee. She ducked back down as Wilder strode towards the car, and Lancing released the air from his lungs in a heavy sigh. He should have known that she wouldn't have the kind of courage it needed to take such a calculated risk.

'He's a touchy bastard,' Craven complained. 'I don't like his attitude.'

'You don't have to,' Rey said. 'He's the big man. He's running the show.'

'Balls. He's just taking orders, like the rest of us.'

'But he's got all the contacts,' Rey reminded him, 'and we can't afford to cross those kind of people. We don't know their faces, but it's sure as hell they'll know ours. Don't push your luck, Joe. It isn't worth it.'

'I don't trust the bastard.' Craven pulled out his knife and polished its blade on the padded shoulder of Lancing's jacket. His voice was sulky.

'I'd like to carve up that pretty-boy face of his . . .'

'Shut your mouth, Craven, you damn fool.' Rey scowled into the rear-view mirror. 'I told you before, I don't like that sort of talk. You can settle with Wilder later, if you really have to, but not on this job. You hear me, Craven? Not on this job.'

Craven slumped back in his seat, still handling the big knife. He was sulking like a spoilt child.

Lancing did not envy Wilder his position as leader of such a precariously balanced outfit. The undisciplined and easily aroused Joe Craven might prove to be the real risk in the operation. As the young gunman's feet pressed uncomfortably into the back of his seat, Lancing realized that the already-established pecking order made him very vulnerable now that Craven's resentments had been brought to the surface. It would be prudent to follow Wilder's example and use Rey as a buffer between himself and Joe Craven.

seven

The southbound carriageway was dotted with fast-moving pairs of lights which penetrated the darkness in crisp white beams. Heavy container-trucks vied for road space with private cars, while overnight buses swayed with every high-speed bend and curve in the road.

Rey drove smoothly, maintaining the gap between his car and the Porsche, and for a long period Lancing was able to relax in his seat with his eyes closed. It was good to take the strain off his neck muscles and let his head rest back against the seat without increasing the pain in his shoulders.

From time to time, Rey glanced at the rear-view mirror. He might have been checking the traffic which flowed in a steady stream of light behind him, or keeping an eye on Craven. After a while, he cleared his throat and spoke quietly to Lancing.

'Tell me about the vault.'

'Huh? What's that?' Caught off guard by the unexpected question, Lancing stammered indecisively.

'I'm asking you what you keep in that vault of yours. What is it that Wilder and his friends are so interested in?'

'Papers . . . that's all . . . just papers.'

Rey's laughter was little more than a low snort. 'Is that what Wilder told you to say?'

Lancing leaned sideways and turned his head, in spite of the pain his movements caused him. He saw that Craven was leaning against one of the rear doors with his feet up on the upholstery and his eyes closed.

'I'm not sure what you're getting at,' he said, carefully, pitching his voice low as he leaned closer to the driver.

'Come off it, Lancing. I'm not that stupid. Nobody keeps a vault like that, with a special time-lock, just for a pile of unimportant business papers.'

'But the vault wasn't my idea. The whole thing was already installed when we took over the building . . .'

'But you *use* it. You take the trouble to set the time-lock for the week-end, even though the shop has a regular alarm system, and you don't even bother to stash away the stuff that's in the upstairs safe. Why? What's down there that's so damn important? According to Wilder, some pretty big people are interested in what you're holding on to, so don't give me all that crap about "just papers".'

Lancing recalled Wilder's threat concerning the secrecy of the vault's contents. He didn't doubt for one moment that the gang's leader intended to carry out his threat if his instructions were disregarded. He had to get Rey off his back, but at the same time he wanted to keep the man interested, to give him something to think about besides his own small share of the raid. A prisoner who might be sitting on a high-profit secret was worth taking extra care of. It wouldn't hurt Rey to suspect that Wilder was on to something big, and that Lancing would gladly tell him all about it, if only he dared.

Lancing shot a glance over the back of the seat, a movement which sent a stab of pain right across his shoulders and up one side of his neck. He was relieved to see that Craven hadn't moved.

'Look . . . er . . .' he stammered deliberately. 'It's like you said before . . . Wilder's running the show . . .'

'And nobody's going to get so much as a sniff inside that vault but him. Is that what you're trying to say?'

Lancing squirmed in his seat. He started to say something, then closed his mouth and groaned aloud. He wanted Rey to think that he was too scared to talk.

'All right, all right,' Rey said impatiently, seemingly convinced by Lancing's act. 'Just tell me one thing. Is it worth it? Is it really worth the risk of hanging around for maybe as long as two nights, just to pick up what's in there?'

'Wilder thinks so.'

'That's not what I want to know.'

Lancing was silent. He let his head fall forward and bit thoughtfully on his lower lip. He knew that Rey was watching him, noting his reactions, looking for signs that he was dealing with an honest man. He was not a difficult man to fool.

Following the tail-lights of the Porsche, Rey eased over and left the carriageway at the next intersection. He adjusted his speed to suit the slower road, and seemed about to resume his conversation with Lancing when Craven suddenly lurched forward and thrust his face between them.

'Nice try, Kev,' he sneered. 'You don't waste much time, do you?'

'What's that supposed to mean?'

'Pumping Lancing the minute Wilder's out of earshot.'

'Just making conversation,' Rey said, evenly.

'Bullshit!' Craven was grinning, but there was little amusement in his voice. 'You're trying to get in on Wilder's scene.'

'I'm *already* in on it, remember?'

'Oh, yes, except that you and me take the same risks for a smaller pay-off, eh, Kevin?' Craven was bouncing gently on the edge of his seat, like a child who was getting excited. He didn't seem to notice that Lancing was edging himself over towards the door, putting as much space as he could between himself and the other two men.

'I just wanted to find out what was involved, that's all,' Rey said.

'And then what?' Craven sneered. 'You could double-cross Wilder . . . kill him . . . take all the stuff for yourself . . . but then what? What the hell would you be able to do with it?'

'Listen, I had no intention . . .'

'You'd be taking on the syndicate,' Craven laughed aloud. 'The whole fucking syndicate . . . you screwball . . . you wouldn't get as far as the end of the street.'

'Craven . . .'

'They'd snuff you out.' Craven used his hands as if he held a machine-gun, and made loud clicking noises between bursts of laughter. 'Bang, bang, you're a dead man.'

'Shut up, Craven.'

'Rat-tat-tat . . . gimme the papers . . . rat-a-tat-tat.'

'Craven!'

The car swerved as Rey yelled Craven's name at the top of his voice. There was instant silence in the back seat.

'Now, you listen to me, Craven,' Rey said, his voice firm but friendly. 'When you're dealing with a man like Vince

Wilder, you can't afford to make that kind of joke. I'm satisfied with my cut. I don't intend trying to doublecross anyone, and I don't give a shit how much Wilder stands to make out of this. I was just curious, that's all, just curious. You got that?'

'Yes, yes. I hear you, Kev.'

'Now forget it, will you? If Wilder gets it into his head that we're trying to make job changes behind his back, he'll blow the pair of us out. I want to get all this over with the minimum of friction, so let's have no more careless talk about cutting out on Wilder. Right?'

'Right.'

Craven pushed his feet into the back of Lancing's seat as he made himself comfortable. He lit a cigarette, tossing the spent match from the partly opened window. He was still chuckling quietly.

Lancing and Rey exchanged glances, and Lancing allowed himself the luxury of a secret smile. He had discovered resentment and suspicion in the two gunmen, and he saw both as chinks in the armour of Vince Wilder.

The smoothness of the ride, and the pleasant breeze on his face lulled Lancing into a state of relaxation. His eyes were heavy, his thoughts drifting, when it occurred to him that the scenery was beginning to look familiar. The huge, darkened supermarket still carried the advertisement for the previous week's 'Monster Sale'. His heartbeat quickened as he scowled at the tail-lights of the Porsche and saw it swing to the right at a wide road junction.

'Where the hell are we going?' he demanded hoarsely.

'Don't ask me.' Rey shrugged.

Craven sat forward in his seat to hear what was said between the other two men. He lurched sideways as the car took a sharp left turn into a tree-lined avenue.

'Jesus Christ,' Lancing groaned.

'What's the matter?' Rey demanded.

'This is Hilltop Avenue.'

'So what? Do you know where we're going?'

Lancing nodded miserably. He felt the skin tighten across

his scalp. Ahead of them, the Porsche swung into the driveway of a house whose terraced lawns were skirted by trees. A cool, scented breeze rustled through the leaves. As the gravelled surface of the drive crunched beneath the tyres of the car, Craven whistled his appreciation of his surroundings.

'The bastard,' Lancing hissed. 'The cunning bastard.'

'Your house,' Rey offered. 'Right?'

'Right,' Lancing confirmed. 'What's so damn funny?'

'The whole thing,' Rey grinned. 'He said we'd hole up in a safe place, and, by hell, he's kept his word. There can't be a safer place in the country than right here, in your own house.'

'He's a bastard.'

'A clever bastard,' Craven corrected.

'And don't you forget it,' Rey said, still grinning. 'That's what makes him the boss and you and me the hired hands.'

They followed the driveway to the large garage at the side of the house. Wilder opened the double doors with a key from Lancing's bunch, then drove the Porsche inside and parked it neatly alongside one wall. Seconds later, Rey pulled into the garage, miscalculated the distance between the two cars, and scraped his nearside against the Porsche, leaving a large groove in the pale blue paintwork.

'Keep the noise down,' Wilder reminded them. 'We don't want the neighbours coming to investigate.'

He helped Shirley from the car and allowed her to stand close to Lancing. She was breathing heavily behind the gag. As she leaned against him, Lancing rested his chin on the top of her head and stared at the silent house. One of the windows of the front bedroom was open, its lace curtains flapping gently. It was unlikely that Catherine would have heard them arrive. The dark green capsules with her bedtime drink were a nightly ritual which assured her of at least seven hours of undisturbed sleep. It was a long time since she had managed to sleep without them.

'My wife isn't up to this, Wilder,' Lancing said. 'She can't cope with this sort of thing. She isn't very strong.'

'In my experience,' Wilder replied, sounding like a friendly family doctor, 'women are never as weak as they would have us believe. I'm sure your wife will cope perfectly well.'

'But the guns will terrify her.'

'Nonsense. Women need to know where they stand. As soon as she sees the guns, she'll know that we mean business and she'll do exactly as she's told. That way, we won't get our lines crossed, and we won't have to teach her the rules of the game, will we?'

Without bothering to relock the garage doors, Wilder herded Lancing and Shirley towards the house. The nearby avenue was deserted, the nearest house in darkness save for its dim porch light. There was no sound other than the crunch of their feet on the ground and the whisper of leaves as they moved in the breeze. The steps leading to the front door were lit by an ornate lamp which hung from a metal wall-bracket. Its light cast grotesque shadows of the group on to the pale walls.

'Which key?' Wilder demanded in a whisper, spreading the bunch across his palm and holding it beneath the light.

'The big one . . . the bronze one with the red tag, but . . .'

'But what?'

'Oh, nothing. Forget it.'

Wilder lifted the shotgun. Its barrel glinted in the light and its shadow appeared on the ground near Lancing's feet.

'But what, Lancing?'

'Maybe my wife bolted the door from the inside. She wasn't expecting me home tonight, and she's usually pretty nervous when she's in the house by herself.'

Wilder stared at him for a long time through narrowed eyes. He seemed to be working out his alternatives.

'Can't we get out of this light?' Rey said. 'It's making me nervous. Look at all these shadows. I bet they can be seen from the other side of the damn road.'

Lancing held his breath as Wilder inserted the key in the lock and turned it firmly. Catherine was a methodical woman. Her daily life seemed to be made up of patterns, neatly-planned events following upon each other in organized simplicity. She would surely have remembered to bolt the doors, as a matter of habit, before going to bed.

The door swung soundlessly open on to the carpeted hallway, and Max Lancing cursed under his breath. He tried not to let his anger show, but his mouth tightened involuntarily, and the very act of trying to control his emotions caused him to raise his head and square his shoulders.

'Now, now . . . temper, temper.' Wilder smiled, pushing the door wide and making a sweeping gesture with his arm as an invitation to Lancing to step inside. 'Don't get mad at the little lady just because she doesn't have your keen sense of security.'

'Maybe that's not what makes him mad,' Craven taunted. 'Maybe your honest shopkeeper suspects that his wife left the door unbolted so that some neighbourhood stud with a duplicate key could come calling on her in the middle of the night. Is that so, Mr Shopkeeper?'

Lancing ignored him and looked instead at Wilder, who stood against the door with his arm still extended. Light from the porch lamp illuminated his features, making his eyes sparkle like dark gems in his handsome face.

'Can we please get out of this light?' Rey's hand was warm-palmed on Lancing's back, easing him forward, into the house. Shirley was pushed close to Craven. She shrank back as he leered at her, his face only inches from her own. The light faded from the hallway with the closing of the door, plunging them into almost total darkness.

'Where are the lights, Lancing?'

'To your left, next to the mirror.'

Wilder's hand skimmed the wall, found the switch and filled the hall with soft, pink-tinted light. He was still smiling at Lancing, his expression unchanged, as he gave the other men their orders in a loud whisper.

Craven and Rey moved quietly from room to room in a swift examination of the ground floor. At last they herded their captives into the sitting-room, where Shirley was pushed towards the sofa and Lancing ordered to sit in a high-backed chair. The curtains were drawn across the wide window, the kitchen blinds closed, the side and front doors bolted. As the gang moved about, handling his property, invading the privacy of his home, Lancing really began to feel like a prisoner. His position, as far as the robbery was concerned, had barely changed, but sitting in his own house, with his hands tied behind his back and armed men walking from room to room, had a very unpleasant effect on him.

He tried not to look at Shirley and not to think of his wife, asleep in the room above them. Wilder had really scored against him this time. Not only had he chosen the safest place in which to hide out until he could complete his job, but he had also made a deliberate move to undermine Lancing's self-confidence. Vulnerability increased with humiliation, and Wilder was not the kind of man to have stumbled across that fact accidentally.

Wilder was watching him from the doorway. He was smiling, closely scrutinizing the other man's face. He pushed what looked like a matchstick, but might have been a wooden toothpick, into his mouth and chewed on it, letting it protrude between his teeth like a cigarette. He nodded his head, clearly satisfied by Lancing's discomfort.

eight

Joe Craven walked around the room, handling its contents. He took two miniature paintings from the wall above the writing-desk, scrutinized the decorative silver frames, then handed them to Rey for his approval. When the other man nodded his head, Craven stuffed the paintings into the bag with the rest of the property stolen from the shop. Lancing was struck by the man's carelessness. Pushed amongst the figurines, goblets, and other bulky items, the unprotected canvases were almost certain to be damaged. Minutes later, several other pieces, including a gold wristwatch and an onyx paperweight, were added to the haul.

'Which bedroom does your wife sleep in, Lancing?'

Wilder leaned over him, speaking in a soft voice and with barely concealed amusement. He was clearly enjoying what he was doing.

'Directly above,' Lancing said. 'The first door at the top of the stairs. Look, Wilder, go easy on her . . .' He stopped, regretting his words. It was not a good idea to ask Wilder for favours; to imply that he could be intimidated through his wife was to invite trouble for them both. Besides, if Catherine Lancing was about to experience the shock of waking to find a gunman in her bedroom, she had only herself to blame. He had always stressed the importance of making sure that the house was secure before retiring for the night, and it was certainly not the first time she had failed to carry out his instructions. She could think herself fortunate if the consequences of her carelessness were robbery, and not murder.

'The first door at the top of the stairs,' he repeated.

Shirley was watching him from the sofa almost opposite his chair, her eyes wide and moist. Mascara had smudged from her eyelashes to leave black rings beneath her eyes, giving her a haggard look. The gag which bit into her already bruised mouth was wet with saliva and stained with lipstick. It had been tied so thoughtlessly that strands of her hair were caught up in the knots. Lancing wondered that he was able to look at her so dispassionately. He felt detached, and vaguely irritated by the way her wide blue eyes seemed to accuse him. He was sorry for the mess they were in, but he didn't consider himself responsible for the way she had been handled and gagged. Her own hysteria had dictated the treatment she received, and only calmer, more sensible behaviour would change that, now. Her gaze flickered from his face to a point just behind him. She drew a deep breath and lifted her head, and for a moment he thought he saw something of the old Shirley in her eyes, cool and haughty.

Catherine Lancing was standing in the doorway, elegantly dressed in a cream silk dressing-gown and high-heeled slippers. She looked round the room, noting the bare surfaces and empty shelves which had so recently housed many personal treasures. Her gaze rested briefly on the other two gunmen, the bulging plastic bag, the casually held weapons. She seemed to take in the whole scene in seconds. As she moved past Lancing, her hand brushed lightly against his shoulder. There was something unexpectedly reassuring for him in her presence: in the smell of her perfume and the faint rustle of her dressing-gown. He watched her sit down on the sofa without so much as a glance at Shirley Foster, her hands clasped in her lap and her face expressionless. He felt an intense, irrational flood of relief. She was unharmed, calm, unafraid, still mistress of her house, in spite of the armed intruders. After twenty-two years of well-planned, beautifully organized domesticity, he almost felt that he could sit back and rely on her to resolve the situation.

Wilder's voice brought him sharply back to reality, reminding him of the seriousness of their predicament.

'I don't like this, any more than you do,' he said, addressing them all. He began tugging at the knots on Shirley's gag, making her wince as her hair became more entangled in the fabric. At last, the grubby handkerchief was unfastened, leaving deep marks on her skin and pulling out several strands of her hair. Wilder tossed the gag aside and scowled at her bruised mouth before continuing.

'I should have been finished with this job hours ago. I hadn't planned on coming here and having to wait for George Warwick to show up with his key.'

He moved round the back of the sofa, touching Shirley's neck and head with the shotgun. Then, watching Lancing all the time, he leaned over and pressed the heavy weapon against Catherine's throat.

'Is there a spare key? Is there any other way to get inside that vault?'

'No,' Lancing said firmly. 'I swear there's no spare key, and no other way to open the door.'

'Is he telling the truth?' Wilder demanded of Catherine, his face very close to hers.

'I know nothing about it. My husband does not discuss his business affairs with me.'

Wilder jerked the shotgun away from Catherine's neck and flopped into a deep leather chair. He was frowning and tired.

After lounging in the chair for a few minutes, he got to his feet and stretched his arms above his head, yawning noisily. Then he picked up the shotgun, which he had placed on the arm of his chair, and spoke sharply to the other two men.

'First we eat, then we sleep. We could be here for another thirty or so hours, so we might as well make ourselves comfortable. We'll take four hours sleep in turn.'

'I'm wide awake,' Rey assured him. 'I don't need my four hours yet.'

'Me neither,' Craven echoed. He was rifling carelessly through the drawers of Lancing's desk.

'All right, I'll take the first period. I'll use one of the bedrooms, and while I'm up there, I don't want either of you interfering with the prisoners. Is that clear?'

'Don't fret about it,' Craven grinned. 'We swear not to kill anyone while you're gone.'

'Just leave them alone,' Wilder insisted, without humour. 'And keep your grubby little hands off the girl.'

'Is that an order . . . sir?'

'That's an order. Do as you're told, and stay out of trouble, Craven. You'll get some action when I say so, and not before. Right . . .' he lifted Catherine Lancing by the arm and pushed her from the room. 'Get in there and make us something to eat, lady.'

He jabbed at her with the shotgun. In spite of her cool composure, Lancing could see that her hands were trembling as the gunman shoved her towards the kitchen.

'Hey, what d'you think he meant by that?' Craven asked his companion in a quiet voice.

'By what?' Rey asked, moving round the back of Lancing's chair as if to follow the other two from the room.

'By that remark about me getting some action, when he says the word.'

'How the hell do I know what he meant?' Rey was craning his neck round the open doorway, obviously trying to keep an eye on what was happening in the kitchen.

'I wouldn't mind a piece of *this* action,' Craven said, his voice thick with insinuation. He was rubbing his palm up and down Shirley's cheek.

'Leave it, Craven. You heard what he said.'

With a quick glance towards the kitchen, Craven bent down and kissed Shirley on the mouth. His left hand pawed at the front of her jacket, while his other hand, still gripping the pistol, pressed across her forehead, pinning her head against the back of the sofa.

'I said, leave it, Craven.' Rey strode across the room and shoved Craven roughly. When the younger man rounded on him, he jabbed his pistol at his belly and ground words through clenched teeth.

'Grow up, you stupid bastard. Don't push your luck with Wilder. If he doesn't put a bullet in your head himself, he can soon find someone to do it for him. He isn't one of your small-time villains, Craven. He's a professional, and he could break a nothing like you without so much as batting an eyelid.' He shoved the gun, sending Craven sprawling back against the wall.

'All right. All right,' Craven protested. 'Cut the rough stuff, will you?' He sounded amiable enough, but his eyes blazed with anger and his smile was strained. He turned away and began tipping out the drawers of a small dresser, sorting through their contents after they had hit the floor, with the toe of his shoe.

Shirley Foster shuddered violently and turned her face into her shoulder, as if trying to rub away the contact of Craven's mouth. Perspiration shone on her forehead, and her cheeks were flushed. Her hair fell in an untidy mass around her face.

'Easy, Shirley . . . easy . . .' Lancing leaned forward on the edge of his seat. He desperately wanted to forestall another of her hysterical outbursts.

She lifted her head and looked at him sharply, her face tight with anger. Knowing that the emotion was provoked by, and aimed at, Joe Craven, he was none the less shocked by the hostility in her eyes. Again he had the impression that she was accusing him of something which was completely beyond his control. He was relieved when she lowered her head and sat still, breathing deeply and evenly.

Lancing watched Shirley for a long time while he listened to the sounds of food being prepared in the kitchen. Her skimpy blue suit was designed to cover, but not hide, her figure. Cut low at the neck, the missing top button allowed the jacket to fall open just wide enough to reveal the swell of her breasts. Her skirt was badly creased, and had hitched up past her knees. From where he was sitting, Lancing could see the darker band of one of her stocking-tops. Above it would be the lacy white suspender belt with matching briefs, which she wore to please him. Her vulnerability filled him with guilt as well as exasperation. He did not want to be responsible for her weakness, or threatened by her dependence on him, yet he knew that, in dressing to please him, she might have made herself irresistible to men like Wilder, Rey and Craven.

Joe Craven still prowled the room in search of anything worth stealing. He had rolled up his small jacket and left it on a shelf by the bookcase. Beside it lay the pistol, its polish dulled by the sweat from his palms. His faded denims were patched on one leg and frayed around the bottoms. Held up by a narrow leather belt, they were stretched out of shape around the seat and across both knees. There was a dark, damp stain under each arm of his T-shirt. He had kicked off his shoes and pushed them under the desk. The musty smell of his feet pervaded the room.

Kevin Rey was sprawled in a chair with his eyes partly closed. His elbow was balanced on the arm of the chair, and he was scraping the nail of his index finger backwards and forwards across his front teeth. He looked thoughtful, as if he had a lot on his mind. He was watching Shirley Foster as she slumped at one end of the sofa, and his face was unreadable.

The high-backed chair afforded some degree of comfort for Lancing's shoulder and neck muscles. He sat well back in his seat, taking full advantage of the firm upholstery as he rested his head back and tried to relax. In spike of his bonds having been slackened, his wrists ached and felt swollen. He was hot, weary, and very thirsty. The middle of his back and the palms of his hands were clammy with sweat, and his head was throbbing. He would have given anything to climb into a soft bed and sleep.

He watched his wife come back into the room pushing a two-tiered trolley stacked with food and drink. As if oblivious to the shotgun aimed at her back, she walked calmly into the centre of the room and began to pour coffee into large mugs. She then seated herself on the edge of the sofa with her hands clasped in her lap. Her fine blonde hair framed her face in a simple, collar-length style. Without make-up, her skin was very pale. Lancing noticed how smoothly the dressing-gown hugged her body, the evenness of its surface broken only by the outline of the nightdress which she wore underneath it.

He stared around the room. The smells of stale sweat, coffee and food mingled in his nostrils. For a moment the scene seemed to take on a vivid, unreal quality. His skin suddenly seemed tight across his face and scalp. He was light-headed. He felt as if he was about to be sick.

The gunmen reached hungrily for the food on the trolley, grabbing at cold chicken, beef, fruit and pickle. Craven tore a chunk of bread from the loaf, smeared it with tomato pickle, and stuffed it into his mouth. He swilled it down with sherry straight from the bottle, then filled his mouth with chicken and corn salad. Sherry dribbled from his chin to his already dirty shirt, and bits of carelessly-held food fell to the carpet around his feet.

'Hey, you thirsty, Lancing?' Craven displayed the contents of his mouth as he spoke. He held out the bottle and grinned. The tinted glass was stained with grease from his fingers.

Lancing nodded.

'Sherry OK?'

'Anything.' Lancing nodded again.

With a broad grin on his face Craven held the bottle above Lancing's head and tipped it so that the dark liquid poured over his hair and down his shoulders. It stung his eyes and ran behind his shirt collar. Craven roared with laughter.

'Go stuff yourself, Craven.' Anger blazed in Lancing. He was immediately grabbed by the front of his jacket and yanked forward in his seat so that their faces were very close together.

'Don't push me, shopkeeper,' Craven growled. 'Don't push me, or I'll break your lousy neck.'

Particles of food escaped from his mouth as he spoke, and he twisted a fistful of Lancing's clothes so tightly that it pressed against his throat.

Enraged and helpless, Lancing filled his mouth with saliva and spat in Craven's face. He was felled instantly by a blow to the jaw which sent him and his chair sprawling. The next thing he knew, Craven was standing over him with his gun in his hand, snarling like an animal. He was being forcibly held in check by Kevin Rey, who had slid his arms under Craven's armpits from behind, and clasped his hands round the back of his neck.

'Stop it,' Wilder barked. 'Leave him alone, Craven.'

'Like fuck I will . . .'

Rey's grip tightened, making Craven yell with pain. Wilder walked over, took the gun which dangled from Craven's limp fingers and waved it in its owner's face.

'I won't warn you again, Craven,' he threatened. 'If you mess up this job for me, I'll blow your crummy little head apart.' He jabbed the gun in the soft flesh below Craven's ear. 'Stay in line, damn you!'

Rey released Craven slowly and warily, only disengaging his grip completely when he was sure that the fit of temper had subsided. Then he righted Lancing's chair and helped him into it.

'Stupid bastard,' he hissed, so quietly that Lancing guessed that he was the only one in the room who heard the words.

Joe Craven jerked two fingers towards Lancing's face and made a sucking noise through his teeth. Then he reached for a fresh bottle of sherry, tore a leg from the cold chicken, and flopped down in an easy chair. He ate noisily, spitting bits of skin and fat on to the carpet. He deliberately tilted the bottle so that its contents trickled out and soaked into the pale velvet cover of the chair. When he had stuffed the last of the chicken meat into his mouth, he tossed the bone over the back of his chair. He wiped his greasy fingers on the gold-coloured velvet, then took a long drink of sherry, letting it run from the corners of his mouth and dribble down his chin. He stared at Lancing and grinned. His tongue moved across his bottom lip from one side of his mouth to the other, and he made sure that Lancing was watching him when he turned his attention to Shirley Foster. He allowed his gaze to wander from her neckline to her legs. His left hand went to his crotch and his fingers began to scratch up and down the zipper. He opened his legs wide, and lifted his hips to display the bulge in his trousers. When he looked at Lancing again, his expression was that of a man who knew that he had already won the game he was playing.

nine

Max Lancing cursed his own hot-headed foolishness. For a moment, he had experienced the pleasure of fighting back, of making some kind of protest against the treatment he was being forced to endure. But that moment had been too brief and too quickly regretted to be worth the effort and the risk involved. His self-indulgent outburst had earned him a bruised jaw and a badly jarred neck, and had instantly transformed him in the eyes of his tormentors from a cooperative prisoner to an unpredictable one. He lowered his gaze from Craven's sneering face. Rey had been right to call him a stupid bastard. His single, miscalculated move had left Craven with a severe case of wounded pride and a score to settle. All he could do now was keep his own temper in check and hope that Wilder was man enough to hold the others in line. If Joe Craven ever got the upper hand, the welfare of the prisoners wouldn't count for anything.

*

Vince Wilder finished his food and dabbed at his mouth with a neatly folded handkerchief before replacing his light-weight leather gloves. He poured himself a cup of coffee, sat back in his chair, and sipped it slowly. Apart from the dark shadow of stubble on his face, he looked as elegant as when he had first entered the shop. His suit was uncreased and his tie smartly knotted. His well-styled hair was still in place, his manner once again casual and relaxed. He hid any weariness he might have been feeling behind an air of practised detachment. Even his gloves seemed to be an integral part of his dress, so that he wore them with style, rather than as an awkward extra.

There was silence in the room, lasting for several minutes, before Wilder got to his feet and replaced his coffee cup. He took a toothpick from his inside pocket and scraped at his teeth, somehow managing to make the act acceptably discreet. Then he stretched his arms above his head and affected a loud yawn.

'I'll grab my four hours now,' he said, checking his watch against the large clock above the fireplace. 'Give me a call at seven-thirty, and don't forget my orders, Craven.'

Craven grinned and continued to scratch at his crotch.

'Keep your hands off the girl,' Wilder reminded him. 'Rey, I'm leaving you in charge. Keep everybody quiet, and let me know if anything happens. Anything at all. All right?'

'All right,' Rey said quietly.

It was with apprehension that Lancing watched Wilder leave the room. He listened to the sounds which came from the bathroom, followed by the slamming of the door to the main bedroom. It did not surprise him that Wilder had rinsed out his mouth and washed before going to bed, though he would not expect the other two gunmen to do the same. A few minutes later, the bedroom door opened again and Wilder padded back downstairs wearing Lancing's carpet slippers. He had removed his jacket and shirt to expose strong shoulders and a muscular, hairy chest. He paused in the doorway and looked briefly at Lancing before crossing the room and taking Shirley Foster by the arm. He pulled her towards him, held her firmly by the shoulders, and after careful examination of her bruised face, kissed her gently on the lips.

Lancing held his breath, his muscles suddenly taut and his thoughts racing. Without moving his eyes from Wilder and Shirley, he knew that the others were watching him, anticipating his reactions.

Catherine was cool, sitting perfectly still and concealing her feelings behind her composure like water currents beneath a still surface.

Kevin Rey was curious, still in the process of weighing up Lancing's personality and uncertain of the role he found himself playing in Wilder's game.

Wilder drew back from Shirley without releasing her. They both looked at Lancing. Wilder's mouth twitched in a lopsided smile as one eyebrow raised itself in a quizzical curve. It was almost as if he was asking Lancing's consent.

Shirley's lower lip was trembling, and her eyes revealed the dread which had flooded through her. They seemed to beg, to demand that he help her, that he do something to put an end to the threat with which she was suddenly faced.

Lancing swallowed with great difficulty. From the corner of his eye, he could see Catherine watching the scene like an uninvolved spectator. If he risked personal injury and humiliation in what he knew would be a vain attempt to help Shirley, Catherine would despise him. He couldn't satisfy them all, but he could easily pull himself apart in the attempt.

Wilder's dark eyes twinkled with amusement. He was looking for Lancing's strengths, as well as his weaknesses, and the expressive face conveyed that he fully appreciated what the other man was going through.

Lancing made his decision, and acted on it immediately by closing his eyes and resting his head against the back of his chair. It was a gesture of acceptance, rather than defeat, of cooperation rather than submission. It would satisfy Wilder, Rey and Catherine, and would ensure, at least for the moment, his own personal safety. He kept his eyes tightly closed until he heard the bedroom door slam.

'How's it feel, Lancing?' Craven's voice was taunting, his words slurred with alcohol. 'How's it feel to know that your woman's up there on the bed with Vince?'

Lancing tried to ignore the man. Outwardly calm, his mind was filled with images of Shirley in the arms of the handsome gunman. He recalled an incident which had taken place months earlier, when he had discovered that Shirley was entertaining a young college lecturer at the flat he rented for her. His jealousy, and her lack of remorse, had resulted in their most violent quarrel. He had struck her several times, and she had retaliated by screaming and throwing things at him. In the midst of his rage, he had found himself making brutal love to her while she wept and struggled beneath him. It had been good for them both, and in spite of her pain and anger, Shirley's passion had been as savagely demanding as his own. Thinking of her now, with Wilder, caused a tightening sensation to spread from his belly to his crotch.

Craven dragged himself from the deep cushioned chair with difficulty, and swayed across the room towards Lancing. His large intake of sherry was beginning to interfere with the focusing of his eyes. He gripped Lancing by the chin with one hand, and held on to the arm of the chair, to steady himself, with the other.

'Wilder's screwing the arse off your woman up there,' he sneered. 'He's got her naked on the bed, and he's doing just what he wants with her. Imagine it, Lancing. All that muscle banging away at your little tart.'

Lancing turned his head to avoid the staleness of Craven's breath. The grip on his chin tightened, yanking his head round with a suddenness which sent stabs of pain through his neck.

'I bet she's loving it, Lancing. I bet she's squirming under Vince like there's no tomorrow.'

Tears of pain and suppressed rage stung Lancing's eyes, but he refused to be baited into retaliation.

'She's loving it,' Craven laughed in his face. 'Your hot-arsed little lady is having the time of her life up there.'

He suddenly pushed himself upright and stood looking down at Lancing. He was swaying on his feet and having difficulty in focusing his eyes. With a snort, he took a few unsteady steps backwards and flopped back in his chair. In a matter of minutes, he was issuing loud, rhythmic snores.

Lancing also slept, heavily and without benefit to his aching body. He awoke to find Kevin Rey standing over him.

'Here, drink this,' the man said, holding a glass of cold milk to his lips. 'You were very restless, and moaning in your sleep. You'd better let me take a look at your neck.'

Lancing leaned forward obediently and gritted his teeth while the strong fingers examined his neck, probing the bruised and swollen muscles.

'You're not very bright, are you?' he asked, without malice. 'You didn't have to get hurt. All you had to do was play it cool to avoid any comebacks from anybody.'

'And you didn't have to hit me so hard,' Lancing complained.

'So what did you expect me to do, give you a friendly tap, just as a warning to behave yourself? This is big business. If you want to risk getting yourself hurt, you shouldn't complain when you have to take the consequences. More milk?'

'Please.'

Lancing drank thankfully, letting the cool milk soothe the dryness in his throat. Then he watched the gunman walk over to the window, lift the edge of the curtain, and peer out into the stillness of the sleeping suburb. He was neither restless nor edgy, yet something about him indicated that he was not exactly comfortable in the circumstances in which he found himself.

The main lights had been switched off, and the room was lit by a large lamp on the desk. Light also streamed in from the hallway, creating misshaped shadows and dark corners. Craven still snored in the armchair, his legs thrust out in front of him and his head supported by one bent arm. There were no sounds coming from the bedroom above their heads.

'May I?' Catherine rose from her place on the sofa and indicated the half bottle of sherry still on the trolley.

Rey turned to look at her and nodded very slightly. His eyes flickered over her body and back to her face with neither appraisal nor disapproval.

'Help yourself, Mrs Lancing.'

'Can I pour one for you?'

'No.' He paused for a moment before adding, politely, 'Thank you.'

Lancing watched Catherine closely as she poured herself a large sherry and returned to her seat. She seemed relaxed, with no trace of weariness in her face or her movements. He had always envied her her insomnia. Any man who could function normally, as she could, on only three or four hours sleep each night, could greatly increase his business activities, especially when handling overseas deals.

She surveyed him over the rim of her glass.

'When all this is over, Max,' she asked suddenly, 'do you think Miss Foster will be able to forgive you for exposing her to such . . . indignity?'

'She's an intelligent woman. She can't blame me for this . . .'

'I didn't hear you protest when that man took her.'

'But you saw how things were. Any protest from me would have been nothing more than an empty gesture.'

Catherine smiled and nodded her agreement. 'I doubt if *she* will appreciate that little scrap of logic.'

Lancing looked at Rey, who had moved away from the window and seated himself on the arm of a nearby chair. He was obviously interested in their conversation. When Lancing looked back at Catherine, he was both surprised and irritated to find that she was still smiling. Her well-manicured fingers held the stem of her glass loosely, and she made small circular movements with her hand, watching the amber liquid as it swished in the glass.

'Do you find it amusing?' he demanded. 'Does this lousy mess we're in strike you as funny?'

She looked up at him without raising her head, so that her eyes appeared much larger than usual.

'Yes, Max, it does,' she said, coldly.

Lancing was stunned. It was as if she had struck him in the face. She had always been there, patient, cooperative, depend-

72

able, no matter what course he decided their lives should take. It had simply never occurred to him that she might withdraw her support, it was unthinkable that she should do so at a time when he needed all the help he could get.

'You can't mean that . . .' he stammered.

'Oh, but I do, Max. I do.'

'But I don't understand. Why?'

Catherine laughed softly as she leaned forward to place her glass on the carpet near her feet. She extended her fingers one by one to mark off each reason as she voiced it.

'Joyce Edmundson, Andrea Tate, Margerita Berran, Jennifer Williamson . . . need I go on?'

Lancing closed his eyes and sighed with relief. If jealousy was the only thing on Catherine's mind, he was sure he could smooth things over.

'They meant nothing to me . . . you know that.'

'Oh?' She tilted her head and smiled without warmth. 'Is that supposed to make me feel better? Should I be delighted that I suffered the hurt and humiliation of all your affairs . . . for *nothing*?'

'Catherine . . .' Lancing wasn't sure what to say. He was too weary to summon up the mental dexterity to engage in this kind of verbal battle.

'There was a time, many years ago, Max, when I might have allowed myself to become involved with another man.' She lowered her voice to little more than a whisper. She picked up her glass and took a small sip of sherry, then ran her finger round the rim of the glass to produce a loud humming sound.

'It would have been so easy,' she said. 'He was young and handsome, and infatuated with me. He was exciting and attentive at a time when you were more interested in your work than your wife. We planned to become lovers . . . it was going to be so easy . . .'

Lancing opened his eyes, but did not turn his head to look at his wife. Instead, he watched Kevin Rey's unreadable face as he listened to Catherine's words.

'We arranged to spend a week-end together while you were away on one of your "business trips" abroad, but at the last

minute, I decided that I really didn't have the right.' She
laughed bitterly. 'I was in love with him, but I was also your
wife, and loving another man did not give me the right to
break my marriage vows. So, I didn't turn up at our rendez-
vous, and I sent no message. When he tried to contact me, I
was unavailable. I was thoroughly and inconsolably miserable,
but I was convinced that I had done the right thing.'

She laughed again, a harsh, unfeminine sound.

'Your "business trip" turned out to be a week-end in Rome
with the wife of one of your associates. I never heard from my
man friend again, and I never met anyone else I could . . .'
She paused, took another sip of sherry, then added, 'That's
just one of the many reasons why I despise you, Max Lancing.'

There was little clarity to Lancing's thoughts. Catherine's
story had confused him, leaving him more aware of emotion
than reason. It mattered to him that his wife was faithful, so
much so that he felt mildly affronted by her revelation. It was
a matter of pride that his very attractive wife had not betrayed
him with another man in twenty-two years of sometimes difficult marriage. At the same time, he was astute enough to
realize that her single, thwarted affair, no doubt glamorized by
the passing of time, had left her with a bitterness which she was
now trying to direct against him. A confession of unfaithful-
ness would, at that moment, have suited him better.

'Are you shocked, Max?' Catherine's voice was mocking.
'Are you outraged by my story, even though you have such a
long list of casual affairs to your credit?'

'They meant nothing to me,' Lancing insisted, without looking at her.

'Do you really expect me to believe that not one of those
women meant anything to you?'

'Not one of them.'

'Well, well, well. After all she's going through on your
behalf, I'm sure Miss Foster will be very happy to hear that.'

Lancing sighed deeply. He was too weary to fight with her.
Kevin Rey had seated himself in the armchair, and was observing them through half-closed eyes, his pistol resting across
his thighs. Craven was still fast asleep, and the house was

silent save for the sound of his snores. There would be time enough, later, to put things right with Catherine. No doubt the abrupt ending of his affair with Shirley Foster would be like soothing balm to her wounded pride. His thoughts of Shirley were like a physical ache. He still wanted her, still found her the most exciting and sexually satisfying woman he had known, but realism was one of his stronger qualities, and he was already facing the fact that their affair would not survive the kind of exposure it was now subjected to.

As he allowed his eyes to close, he was already holding Shirley in his imagination, loving her, possessing her for the last time. The instant stirring of need inside him told him that it would not be easy, no matter what was at stake. In spite of everything, he knew that he was not yet ready to give her up.

ten

Lancing's sleep was already disturbed by cramp in his arms when he became aware of sounds from upstairs. He strained his ears in the darkness and heard Wilder using the lavatory. Then he identified the sounds of gargling and spitting in the sink, and the splashing of shower water, followed by the familiar buzzing of his own electric shaver. Some time later, Wilder returned to the bedroom and closed the door behind him.

Lancing was not pleased by what he heard. The implications were that Shirley had pleased Wilder so much that he was going back for more. She might have tried to repel him in the beginning, only to find herself unwillingly aroused by his obvious physical charms. She might even have welcomed him with open arms, subscribing to the old belief that if rape is inevitable, a woman might just as well lie back and enjoy it. Shirley could be quiet and submissive or aggressively demanding, depending on her mood, and Lancing found her equally desirable, whichever type of partner she chose to be. He found himself wondering which facet of her sexual nature Wilder would have most appreciated.

At that moment, Craven hauled himself from his chair and staggered across the room. One hand clutched at his belly, while the other grabbed at furniture for support. He swayed to one side near the door, and fell against the bookcase, knocking a half-dozen books and glass ornaments to the floor. With a loud curse, he flung himself round the door frame and lurched upstairs. The moment he opened the bathroom door, he began to vomit noisily, and it was clear from the sounds he made that he had failed to reach the lavatory pan in time. He stood in the doorway, retching and coughing, before stumbling back downstairs and aiming his body at the chair. Particles of food clung to his chin and shirt-front and glistened on the back of his hand where he had wiped it across his mouth.

Lancing turned away with a shudder of revulsion. Whatever was taking place in the bedroom, he was grateful that it had been Wilder and not Craven who had put claim on Shirley.

Wilder came down from the bedroom with a towel wrapped around his shoulders to protect his clothes from the dampness of his recently-shampooed hair. He was wearing one of Lancing's more expensive shirts, and the neat appearance of his jacket and trousers showed that he had hung them up before getting into bed. He looked cheerful and relaxed, like a man who had just emerged from a long and easy night's sleep.

Shirley Foster followed him into the room, her hands untied and her face pale behind the smudged make-up. She did not look in Lancing's direction, nor did she acknowledge anyone else in the room as she resumed her place at one end of the long sofa. With her elbow propped on the well-padded arm, she let her head fall forward until it rested on her hand, thus concealing her face behind her tangled hair.

Lancing stared at her, searching for fresh marks or bruises on her skin to indicate that she had tried to protect herself against Wilder. He found none. Her fingernails appeared to be intact, her clothes unsoiled, her stockings unsnagged. How-

ever distasteful her encounter might have been, however reluctantly she might have succumbed to the gunman's advances,
Lancing could find no outward sign of rape.

'I hope you don't object to me using your private property,'
Wilder said with mock politeness, as he buttoned the cuffs of
the neatly tailored shirt. He ran his hands across his chest
until his fuzz of dark hair was visible through the fine fabric.
'It's a good fit . . . well put together . . . a pleasure to have next
to my skin.'

Rey snorted softly and shook his head from side to side. His
roughened palm scraped noisily across the stubble on his chin.

'You can have your property back when I've finished with
it,' Wilder continued. The expression on his face said that he
knew Lancing had grasped the double meaning in his words.

'Slightly soiled, perhaps, but none the worse for the experience.'

Lancing eyed Wilder with a defiant stare. He would not
allow the man's taunts to interfere with his self-control. If he
was to salvage anything from the mess he was in, it would only
be done by meeting Wilder on equal terms. Recognizing that
the man hated him, and not having the slightest idea why, he
knew that he must somehow find a way to temper that hatred
with respect.

When Wilder ordered Catherine into the kitchen to make
fresh coffee, she obeyed only after fixing him with a stare of
open contempt. Far from annoying him, her hostility seemed
to afford him some amusement.

'Hey, Kevin,' he called back from the doorway. 'There's a
cloakroom down the hall next to the back door. How about
taking the lady down there so that she can freshen herself up?'

Rey heaved himself from the chair and stretched his arms
above his head as he yawned. Lack of sleep had caused a slight
puffiness around his eyes. He snapped off the desk lamp, then
pulled back the curtains, ignoring the decorative pulley system
which was there for just that purpose. Sunlight streamed in
through the window, promising another hot day.

Without a word, Rey gripped Shirley by the arm, lifted her
from her seat, and steered her from the room. From where

Lancing was sitting, he could watch them pass the open kitchen door and carry on down the short hallway towards the back door. Rey propped himself against the wall just within Lancing's range of vision. He allowed Shirley the privilege of closing the cloakroom door behind her, but his outstretched foot made sure that the door would not close fully, so preventing it from being locked.

Across from Lancing, the younger gunman still snored in the armchair. The abandoned sherry bottle lay on the floor, having slipped from his fingers and tipped the remainder of its contents on to the carpet in a large stain. Propped between his leg and the cushioned arm of the chair, his pistol pointed ineffectually at the far wall. It looked no more sinister than a realistic toy. Lancing discarded the idea of making a grab for the gun almost as soon as it occurred to him. He could not move from the chair without being seen from the hall, and with his hands tied behind his back, possession of the gun would serve no purpose.

Sounds from the kitchen drew his attention. He thought he heard a slap, followed by Wilder's raised voice telling Catherine to keep her mouth shut. He guessed that his wife had voiced some protest about the invasion of her home by the gang. She came from the kitchen carrying a pot of steaming coffee which seemed to fill the room with its aroma. Her face was slightly flushed and her eyes bright, but she showed no sign of being intimidated by the intruders.

Wilder had combed his hair into its sleek style and replaced his leather gloves. He looked up from pouring the coffee as Rey led Shirley back into the room. She had cleaned all the old make-up from her face, leaving her skin pale and lips colourless. The tangles had been smoothed from her hair, and the application of soap and water had done much to lessen the vividness of the marks on her face. She strode into the room almost defiantly, accepted the cup of coffee from Wilder's outstretched hand, and returned to her seat with a toss of her head.

Lancing had a sudden urge to take her in his arms and hold

her against him. She was being brave, coping with a difficult situation with as much calmness and common sense as she possessed. It would have been a great comfort to him to embrace her and let her closeness wipe out the memory of the last few hours completely. He was disappointed when her gaze at last met his. The coldness was still there, like an accusation, in her blue eyes.

Lancing was grateful when the necktie fell away from his wrists. He acknowledged Rey's assistance with a brief nod of his head, then stretched out his arms in front of him, flexing his fingers and rotating his hands at the wrists. He stood up slowly, both to avoid sudden strain to his stiff muscles, and to prevent his captors becoming agitated. On Wilder's instructions, he dialled George Warwick's number, and was not surprised that there was no reply. There were twenty-four more hours before the time-lock on the vault released itself. Another day and another night in the hands of the three criminals. Surely, with all that time in which to think, he should be able to work something out, make a deal, do something to preserve at least a part of his fortune. As he replaced the receiver and moved to the trolley to help himself to food and drink, his mouth was set in a hard, determined line. He had just twenty-four hours in which to come up with something which would tip the scales in his favour.

Joe Craven's rhythmic snores became intermittent. He moved about in his chair, stretching his limbs and turning his head from side to side. He seemed cramped and uncomfortable from lying too long in the same position. He groaned and muttered, licking his lips and grimacing as if he had an unpleasant taste in his mouth. Lancing willed him to remain sleeping. Wilder and Rey he could cope with, but the easily provoked Craven was a very different threat. He watched him wipe his nose with the back of his hand, and once again found himself hoping that Wilder could maintain his leadership.

Craven opened his eyes and sat up in his chair. His hands went to his head and he groaned. After clearing his throat offensively, he spat the contents of his mouth into a corner and reached for a cigarette.

'*Must* you do that?' Wilder snapped.

'Get stuffed,' Craven growled, and spat a second time. 'Christ Almighty, my head aches.'

Wilder jerked his shotgun in the direction of the kitchen and Catherine, immediately understanding his meaning, slipped quietly from the room. She returned with a glass of water and two large, white tablets, which she held out gingerly.

'Here, take these. They'll make you feel better.'

'Huh?' Craven scowled up at her. His eyes were heavy and bloodshot, and a layer of coarse, black stubble covered his cheeks and chin.

'Get stuffed,' he said, drawing deeply on his cigarette.

'Take them,' Catherine repeated, softly. 'They'll cure your headache.'

'I said, get stuffed, you stupid old cow.' With one sweep of his hand, he sent glass and tablets flying across the room.

Catherine drew back, startled by the unexpected violence. Without turning her back on him, she edged her way back to her seat.

'I want the girl.' Craven's voice was a snarl. His eyes were narrowed against the coil of smoke which drifted up from the cigarette at the corner of his mouth.

'No,' Wilder said simply.

'Stuff you, Wilder. I fancy a screw, and I want the girl.'

'No,' Wilder repeated. His voice was cold. His fingers rested lightly on the shotgun at his side.

Lancing stiffened. He saw Rey's hand cover the handle of his pistol in anticipation of trouble. Shirley recoiled, seeming to shrink against the cushioned sofa, the fingers of one hand covering her mouth.

'You've already had her,' Craven spat. 'It's my turn now.'

'No, it isn't,' Wilder disagreed.

'I think it's mine,' Rey cut in, holding his pistol in his left hand and polishing it with his handkerchief, an action which brought the barrel, by accident or design, in line with Craven's head.

'Who says I have to stand third in line?' Craven demanded, his face contorted petulantly.

'I do, Craven,' Wilder said.

'And me,' Rey echoed.

It was a show of strength, a clear indication that, if Craven wanted to change the rules, he would have to go through both men to do it.

Craven lurched to his feet, one hand still nursing his aching head. He adjusted the heavy knife which was pushed down his belt, then opened his mouth and forced out a loud burp.

'Stuff you,' he muttered to himself. He grabbed a bottle from the trolley and took a long gulp, screwing up his face in an expression of distaste as the fiery liquid hit the back of his throat. Then he replaced the bottle and swayed towards the door leading to the stairs. He paused in front of Lancing, glared at him, then lashed out suddenly with his foot and kicked his shin. He roared with laughter, kicked out at the other leg, missed and staggered to one side. He was still laughing as he climbed unsteadily up the stairs, but his laughter turned to curses when he reached the bathroom and was confronted by his own vomit.

'He spewed all over the bathroom floor while you were in the bedroom,' Rey explained. 'He doesn't like having to walk in it to get to the lavatory. I always thought pigs were happy to grovel in their own filth. Craven must be the exception which proves the rule.'

Wilder strode across the room and picked up Craven's pistol, which had been left in the armchair. He removed the bullets and dropped them into his jacket pocket.

'I could have done without him on this job,' he said angrily. 'He's trouble, nothing but trouble.'

'You insisted on a third man . . .'

'Did you have to pick Craven?'

Rey shrugged his shoulders. 'You know he wasn't my original choice,' he reminded Wilder. 'How was I to know that Bailey would get himself arrested at the last minute? Under the circumstances, I was lucky to get *anyone*. If you wanted something better, you should have picked your own man.'

'I told you to find a nobody, some jerk off the streets who wouldn't ask questions and wouldn't be connected with us if the police picked him up. The streets are full of nothings who could have done this job, and you have to pick out an arsehole like him.'

Rey faced Wilder with a steady stare. 'You could have picked your own man,' he repeated. 'What the hell did you want him for, anyway? We don't even *need* a third man.'

'Tactics,' Wilder said, patiently. He pushed Craven's pistol back between the cushion and the arm of the chair. 'Every team needs a fall-guy, a sacrificial lamb, if you like.'

'What the hell for?'

'In case things don't work out as planned, Kevin. We may need a dupe, a decoy . . .' He spread his hands wide, and seemed surprised that Rey should need an explanation.

'When you run the risk of being attacked by wolves, it's a matter of common sense to make sure you have some tasty titbit to throw to the pack so that you can get the hell out of it while they're otherwise occupied.'

Rey stared back at him, his face, as always, devoid of expression. He finally nodded and licked his lips.

'You mean, Craven's the shit?'

'I would have thought that was pretty obvious.'

'And what about me?' Rey's voice gave no indication of his mood.

'What about you?'

'I get the same as Craven, remember? It's a two-way split, equal shares between him and me. So, if he's the shit, what does that make me?'

Wilder's eyes narrowed as he stared at Rey.

'We'll work something out,' he said, after a short pause.

'I think we'd better, Vince.'

They were still facing each other when Craven lumbered back into the room, unaware that he had barged in on their conversation.

Lancing felt that he had witnessed something to his advantage. Twenty-four hours of close contact, perhaps with a little well-timed help from him, could see the two stronger men competing for leadership, and his own personal position greatly strengthened.

He watched Joe Craven help himself to food from the trolley. The cocky, uncouth young man lacked the intelligence to realize that he was held in contempt by his colleagues. As far as Lancing was concerned, Wilder's tactics were far from unfamiliar. He had used the same ploy himself, many times, in his business dealings. On more than one occasion, he had taken the added precaution of actually setting up the third man from the start of the deal. In a tricky situation, it was much easier to get out from under if the hired dupe was busy in the front line, keeping the opposition occupied.

Lancing averted his gaze as Craven looked in his direction, reluctant to have accidental eye contact misinterpreted as open challenge. He would keep out of Craven's reach, and concentrate on strengthening his position with the other two men.

He looked at Catherine and Shirley, sitting one at either end of the long sofa. The deep velvet cushions were no indication of the real distance between them, in spite of the fact that they shared the same man. They both stared back at him, now, without the slightest sign of warmth or affection in their faces. Only a few hours earlier, their attitudes would have troubled, perhaps even distressed him, but now there were much greater issues at stake. If he was to survive the next twenty-four hours, he had to keep his priorities in the right order.

eleven

Vince Wilder ran a comb through his hair and shook his head vigorously. The glossy brown mane fell back into place immediately. He studied his face in the mirror, examined his tongue, picked a minute particle of food from his teeth, then settled himself on a corner of the desk to clean and file his nails.

Lancing stared at the man's hands. Unblemished, and with well-manicured nails, they were strong and steady, the kind of hands which might handle, with equal confidence, a priceless diamond, a woman, or a loaded shotgun. He was still staring at the hands when their movements ceased, leaving the slender fingers poised in mid-air. He looked at Wilder's face and was surprised to find him watching him, his face tilted so that his dark eyes appeared almond shaped. His mouth lifted at one side, stretching into a slow, lop-sided smile. His gaze was penetrating, his eyes creased and bright with amusement. Lancing dropped his eyes to the man's mouth, saw the pink-tipped tongue slide from one side to the other to moisten the smiling lips. A memory stirred in him, a hazy recollection of husky laughter and soft, straw-blond hair. He saw the smile widen, anticipated the even-toothed grin which shaped a deep groove in each cheek.

Lancing jerked his gaze away from Vince Wilder's face. A muscle in his neck throbbed painfully, and the skin across his cheekbones felt tight and hot. He stared at the floor, disturbed by his own embarrassment.

When he looked up again, Kevin Rey was watching him closely. His face revealed nothing of what might be going on in his mind, but something in his eyes demanded caution. He looked at Wilder, who had returned to the task of filing his fingernails, then back at Lancing. Even without words or facial expression, he managed to suggest that he did not like what he was involved in.

Wilder slipped the nail file back into his pocket and replaced his gloves. Then he picked up the telephone and dropped it into Catherine Lancing's lap, startling her.

'Keep dialling Warwick's number,' he ordered, 'and don't try anything silly.'

Catherine glared at Wilder as she dialled, fearlessly expressing her dislike of him. Her attitude provoked him.

'I'm so sorry if this set-up doesn't meet with your approval, Mrs Lancing,' he said, sarcastically.

Catherine fixed him with a steady stare, but said nothing.

'Is it the guns that upset you? The mess? The presence of your husband's *young* lady?' He heavily emphasized the word 'young'.

'You're an animal,' Catherine told him. She let the receiver fall back into its cradle and tossed her head, facing him defiantly.

'Really?' he asked, leaning over the back of the sofa. 'Am I to assume, by that statement, that you disapprove of my . . . er . . . liaison with Miss Foster?'

'You're an animal.'

'And you're number two in the desirability ratings, Mrs Lancing,' Wilder spat.

Catherine drew in her breath sharply, shocked by his cruelly personal remark.

'You should be pleased,' he mocked her, leaning closer. 'You should be thanking me, instead of dishing out insults. You admit that you hate your husband, so what the hell have you got to complain about? Doesn't it please you to see him on his knees? Doesn't it give you a deep sense of self-righteous satisfaction to see him and his tart getting no more than they deserve?'

'Stop it!' Catherine hissed. 'Stop it!'

'You can't have it both ways. What part do you want to play in this little drama, high-minded lady, or vengeful wife?'

Catherine swung her arm in an attempt to slap the gunman's face, but he caught her by the wrist and forced her hand back towards her shoulder, making her wince with pain. They both ignored the telephone, which clattered to the floor at her feet.

'Don't push me, lady,' Wilder warned, his face very close to hers. 'This show is *mine*.' He jerked his thumb against his chest, his eyes blazing. 'It's *mine*, and *nobody* is going to tell me how to run it.'

He shoved her from him and turned his back on her, moving stiffly away from the sofa. His anger had flared suddenly and unexpectedly, and the tension in his body showed that it was not yet spent. He spasmodically clenched and unclenched his fists, and only after a series of deep, controlled breaths did his outward calm return. He was smiling again when Kevin Rey offered him a fresh cup of coffee some minutes later.

The clock above the fireplace had stopped a little after nine o'clock when Lancing awoke from a heavy sleep. He had the uneasy impression that he had been muttering while he slept, but a quick glance around the room told him that nobody was paying the slightest attention. He felt groggy and very uncomfortable. His mouth was dry, with a stale taste which he found unpleasant. He surveyed the other occupants of the room through half-closed eyes, so as not to draw attention to himself.

Catherine was once again sitting with the telephone balanced on her knee. She looked tired and drawn. At the other end of the sofa, Shirley sat with her head bowed. Her shoulders rose and fell gently as she breathed. She moved in her sleep, turning her lovely, bruised face in his direction, and Lancing looked quickly away, feeling guilty.

Wilder was standing at the window with a foot resting on the polished top of a low cupboard. He was holding his shotgun lightly in one hand, letting it swing to and fro, brushing his thigh in a gentle, swinging motion. His face was still, save for the occasional movements of his jaw as he shifted the matchstick which he held in his teeth. Beyond the lace-patterned drapes, there was little for him to see which might be of interest. The rolling lawns and flower beds, the tidy outline of neighbouring houses, and the carefully planned impressions of space, were designed to relax, rather than stimulate. In spite of this, the man seemed perfectly content to stand at the window, his attention drawn beyond the quiet room.

Kevin Rey had fallen asleep in his chair. For the first time, Lancing could see that the watchful grey eyes were actually closed and the big hands relaxed. His mouth was slightly open, but his slow, even breathing was soundless.

'Hello? Hello?' Catherine Lancing's voice shattered the silence in the room. '. . . er Mr Warwick, please . . . let me speak to Mr George Warwick.'

Wilder crossed the room in a few strides and pressed the shotgun against the side of Catherine's neck, a chill reminder that her life was threatened. She covered the mouthpiece with her hand and spoke to Wilder in a loud whisper.

'He's not back yet, but she expects him very soon. Do you want him to ring us?'

'Who's that?' Wilder mouthed.

'His daughter.'

Wilder nodded his head sharply, and Catherine returned to her rather stilted conversation.

'Ask him to ring his partner,' she instructed. 'It's a matter of the greatest urgency. Please ask him to contact Mr Max Lancing the moment he returns . . . it's terribly urgent.'

She lowered the receiver and closed her eyes, releasing the air from her lungs in a long sigh.

With a smile of satisfaction, Wilder replaced the telephone on the desk and winked at Rey, who had opened one eye in response to the interruption.

Lancing's thoughts were confused. He had hoped to avoid making contact with George, thereby forcing Wilder to take the risk of robbing the vault in broad daylight on a busy working day. By then, he might have managed to work out some kind of deal with the gang, or at least be in a position to bargain. Once Wilder got that other key, there was nothing to stop him going ahead with his plans to ruin Lancing. He cursed under his breath. Damn George Warwick! He needed more time.

'I found some more things worth having,' Craven announced, tossing an armful of the Lancing's personal belongings to the floor. He grabbed the plastic bag and inverted it, tipping out the contents. Muttering loudly to himself, he got down on his knees and began to divide the items into two untidy piles. During the process, a gold bracelet and two diamond rings found their way into the back pocket of his denims. As he handled the goods, he cast furtive glances towards the other two men. He was obviously accustomed to his actions being observed with suspicion.

'Don't take that!' Catherine Lancing's voice was loud and sharp. It brought the gunman's muttering to an abrupt end and caused him to turn his head slowly and look at her with a sneer. When she saw his face, she realized that she had spoken hastily. She lowered her voice and addressed him again, her tone greatly altered.

'Please, don't take the picture, Mr Craven. It's the only one I have . . . it's irreplaceable. Take the frame . . . it's solid gold . . . but please leave the picture.'

Lancing groaned inwardly. Craven was not the sort of man who would respond favourably to even the mildest show of distress. In trying to appeal to the better side of his nature, Catherine was likely to bring out the worst in him.

Craven stared at the portrait in its neat frame. A dark-haired boy of about three years old laughed back at him from the faded photograph.

'My son . . . our little boy,' Catherine explained softly. 'There was an accident. He was killed. The picture is all we have left.'

Craven stared at the photograph for a long time before removing it from the frame, which he dropped on to one of the piles of valuables at his feet. Then he perched on the arm of the nearest chair and stared at Lancing and the face of the boy in turn.

'Your boy?' he asked at last.

'Yes.' Lancing nodded.

'Dead?'

Lancing nodded again.

'How?'

'Drowned.'

'How old was he?'

Lancing noticed that Catherine's fingers were plucking nervously at her handkerchief. He would have been happy to let Craven take the picture. It was the kind of mute, faded reminder that he could do without.

'He was almost four when it happened,' he said. 'It was his first sailing trip. There was a sudden storm, and Robert was washed overboard.' It was a practised answer, perfected over the years to give maximum explanation with the minimum of intrusion into his privacy.

'Whose fault was it?' Craven demanded.

'Fault? It was nobody's fault. Like I said, the storm came up suddenly. It couldn't have been foreseen. It was nobody's fault.'

'I mean,' Craven said, deliberately, 'who was responsible for the kid? Whose boat was it? Who took him sailing in the first place? *Someone* must have been responsible for such a small kid.'

There were tears in Catherine Lancing's eyes. After sixteen years, she was crying because Robert's memory had been disturbed.

'I was,' Lancing said.

'Oh, so it was *you* who killed him?' Craven was grinning, and Lancing knew that he was being baited.

'I didn't kill him. It was an accident,' he said, mildly.

'I bet your wife doesn't agree with that. And I bet you were so busy screwing away from home that one kid is all you managed to make. That right, Lancing?'

'That's not true . . .'

'Oh? So, how many kids have you?'

Lancing stared at the gunman's soiled shirt. He wanted to end the discussion, but he didn't know how.

'How many?' Craven repeated.

'Just one. Just Robert.'

Craven whistled through his teeth and drummed his fingers on the face in the photograph.

'That's some crud you're married to, lady,' he said to Catherine. 'Here, you want your picture back?'

Catherine reached out for the precious reminder of her dead child. Craven allowed her fingers to touch it before snatching it away and holding it above his head. His laughter was cruel.

'Give it back,' Wilder said.

'Oh, come on,' Craven complained sulkily. 'It's only a fucking old photograph.'

89

'Give it back.'

Craven held the photograph in both hands.

'In one piece,' Wilder said quickly. 'And do it *now*.'

The photograph fluttered into Catherine's lap. She touched it with her fingers, closing her eyes and allowing a tear to run unheeded down her face. Her grief was something Lancing could not really understand. After sixteen years, he felt that he would have to dig very deeply inside himself to find any real pain, even though he had loved his son dearly. Yet Catherine's eyes could brim with tears at the mention of his name. He recalled how, a full year after the accident, he had felt compelled to clear the house of every reminder of the boy. He had burned his toys and his clothes, destroyed pictures, furniture, bedding. He could no longer live with the constant reminders which, he was convinced, were keeping his wife's wounds open and raw. Weeks later, Catherine had regained some of her lost composure, and the incident had not been referred to since. It seemed incredible to him that she could appear to be so fearful of losing her son, when in actual fact, she had lost him all those years ago.

Rey heaved himself to his feet and flexed his shoulders. His body was wide and solid, and his trousers stretched across powerful thighs. He stood for a minute with his fists on his hips, then nodded solemnly at Wilder. He turned his head without moving his body, so that he could look at Lancing from the corners of his eyes. He was frowning slightly. He nodded his head again, then stepped forward and stood before Catherine Lancing, one hand outstretched.

It was some time before Catherine realized what the man's intentions were. She looked up at his expressionless face and her eyes widened. She jerked her head round to stare at Wilder, who returned her stare before turning back to look out of the window.

'Mrs Lancing?' Rey's voice was quiet. He snapped the fingers of his outstretched hand, then held it palm uppermost, waiting.

'No . . . no . . .' She looked back at Wilder as if appealing for help, but he appeared to have lost interest in what was happening in the room.

'Mrs Lancing,' Rey said again. 'Come on. Don't give me any trouble.'

'You can't . . .'

Ignoring her protests, Rey reached down and took her by the arm, lifting her effortlessly to her feet.

'Hey, Kev, you sure you really fancy the old one?' Craven called, grinning.

Rey ignored him as he steered Catherine towards the stairs.

'Kinky bastard,' Craven laughed. He was leaning against the wall with one foot on the arm of a chair and a partly smoked cigarette hanging limply from one corner of his mouth. He was scratching his crotch and eyeing Shirley Foster. When he glanced across at Lancing, it was to give him a knowing wink. As far as he was concerned, he was next in line for the bedroom.

twelve

Joe Craven found a large, draw-string bag in which to place his share of the stolen goods. He took advantage of Rey's absence by lifting a few items from his pile of valuables and pushing them in with his own. Even after he had fastened the bag and carefully laid it in a corner near the door, he couldn't resist returning to Rey's share, picking out a gold signet ring, and placing it on his own finger. He strutted round Lancing's chair, observing him with an air of self-importance.

Lancing kept his gaze on the carpet in front of him. He felt that to look Craven directly in the eye when there was so much hostility between them, would be like an open challenge. A man with such a hair-trigger temper had to be handled with caution.

Craven waited until Wilder had turned back to the window before he leaned over and pulled both Lancing's hands behind his back, binding them tightly together with the discarded necktie. Then he stood back to admire his handiwork. He seemed disappointed that, apart from a wince as the pressure was first applied to his wrists, his victim made no form of protest.

Moving away from Lancing, he paced the floor as if looking for something to occupy him. He glanced at his watch and yawned, then ground his cigarette stub into the empty packet and tossed it against the wall. Boredom was beginning to eat away at his temper. There was no more liquor in the house, and he had just smoked his last cigarette. He wandered restlessly into the kitchen and proceeded to search the cupboards and the refrigerator. The next few hours were going to be hell, unless Wilder and Rey could control their quicksilver companion.

'You'll never keep a grip on that kid,' Lancing said, quietly.

Wilder turned slowly and fixed him with a confident smile.

'Are you counting on that?' he asked.

'You know me better than that . . .'

'Oh, yes, I do.'

Lancing ignored the interruption. A glance towards the kitchen told him that Craven was busy trying to prise open a carton of fruit juice, but he still took the precaution of lowering his voice.

'He'll fuck this job up for you, if you're not careful, and he'll probably take us all down with him. He's already got his own share, and he's not going to give a toss if you don't get yours.'

'Is that so?'

'You know he's trouble,' Lancing insisted. 'He'll slit your throat just to show you how sharp his knife is.'

'Are you telling me that I don't know what I'm doing, Lancing? That I can't handle this?'

'I hope you can, because if you get careless, he'll have us all in shit street.'

He could hear water running in the kitchen. Something heavy, like a saucepan, fell to the tiled floor.

'Call it off,' he whispered, urgently. 'Let them take their share and get them both off your back.'

'You must think I'm stupid . . .'

'A deal, Wilder. Some kind of deal, without all this. It's too messy . . . too risky . . .'

'What kind of deal did you have in mind?'

At that moment, Craven came back into the room with a large piece of sweet cake in his hand and his dark moustache dotted with cream.

'Get lost, Craven,' Wilder snapped.

'Huh?'

'I said, get lost. Go see if you can find anything valuable in any of the other rooms.'

'But I already looked . . ' he frowned at Wilder, then went back to his cake.

'Out!' Wilder ordered, and with no more than a brief shrug of his shoulders, Craven ambled from the room.

'Now, Lancing, what's the deal?'

'Why don't you work one out on your own terms?' Lancing offered, carefully. He wasn't sure how much Wilder knew, and he wanted to avoid committing himself more than was necessary. There was no point in bargaining for a quarter of a million in cash *and* the diamond shipment, if Wilder might be prepared to settle for one or the other. He didn't even consider his records-book in his plan.

'Anything you say,' he added. 'Name your price.'

'You're a cool one, Lancing,' Wilder smiled. 'But then, you always were. Did you really think that I'd fall for that move a second time?' He made small clicking noises with his tongue and waved his fingers in front of his face. 'Come now, Max, old friend. Whatever you may think of me, I assure you, I'm not that stupid.'

Voices reached them from upstairs, followed by the slamming of a door and the soft pad of footsteps on the stairs. Kevin Rey appeared in the doorway, bare-footed, and with his shirt flapping open. A purple scar snaked across his chest from shoulder to navel, and a smaller one sat like a second nipple on his left breast. He took in the scene through narrowed eyes.

'What's going on here?' he asked.

Wilder raised an eyebrow and tilted his head, a quizzical expression on his face.

'What kind of question is that?' he countered.

'Craven says you were talking with Lancing. He says you sent him out of the room so you could talk privately.' Rey eyed each man in turn, as poker-faced as ever in spite of the charged situation.

'It was nothing . . .'

'Shut your mouth, Lancing,' Wilder barked.

Lancing had no more to say. His hasty protest had been designed to confirm the other man's suspicion that something was being worked out in his absence.

'There's nothing to get excited about,' Wilder said, calmly. 'I'm here to take what I want, not to make deals.'

'Then why the privacy? Why get rid of Craven?'

'Because that crud gets on my nerves, that's why.' There was irritation in Wilder's voice as he skilfully directed the aggravation back at Rey. 'You brought Craven on this job, so don't expect me to play nursemaid to him while you're enjoying yourself in the bedroom.'

Rey stood for a moment looking back at Wilder. Then, with a glance at Lancing which told him nothing, he left the room as silently as he had entered it.

Joe Craven stood aside to allow him to pass, then walked into the room with a sheepish smile on his face. He seemed pleased that he had managed to cause friction between the two men.

The incident left Wilder looking slightly unnerved. He stayed close to the window, grinding his teeth and scowling at the deserted lawns beyond the glass.

Craven aimed his knife at the desk and cursed when it struck the polished top and bounced to the floor. He retrieved it, took more careful aim, and threw it again. This time, the point of the blade penetrated the wood and the knife remained upright, quivering. He grinned and tried again, proud of his accuracy and delighted with his new game. The repetitive thud as the knife hit the desk reminded Lancing that he still had a throbbing headache.

When Rey came back into the room, his clothes were intact and his face freshly shaven. He led Catherine politely by the arm, only releasing her when she was reseated on the sofa. She raised her head and stared steadily at her husband. Her hair was untidy, her eyes bright, the paleness of her cheeks highlighted by the deep flush on her cheekbones. With her lips slightly parted, she held her head proudly and glared at her husband until he turned away from her.

Craven sniffed noisily as he wiped his nose with the back of his hand. He pushed his knife down the waistband of his trousers and grinned at Rey.

'About time,' he said, licking his lips.

Lancing braced himself, knowing what was on the gunman's mind.

As Craven reached for Shirley, she shrank back, covering her face with her hands. He grabbed her wrists and yanked her to her feet.

'Stop it,' Wilder ordered. 'Leave the girl alone, Craven.'

'For fuck's sake . . .' Craven shoved Shirley so hard that she fell heavily, striking her head on the back of the sofa.

'You're out of line, Wilder.'

'What did you say?'

'I said, you're out of line. You might be running this job, but you've pushed me around enough. I want the girl, and I'm going to have her.'

'Like hell you are, Craven.' Wilder's fist was fast and accurate. It caught Craven on the edge of his jaw, snapping his head back and sending him crashing to the floor. As he reached for his gun, Rey's foot stamped down on his fingers, pinning both hand and weapon the floor. He grabbed Rey's ankle with his free hand, snarling furiously, but was unable to shift the weight of the heavier man.

'You're taking orders from *me*,' Wilder reminded him, his

face tight with anger. 'You do as I say, when I say it. Is that clear?'

Craven clenched his teeth and renewed his efforts to free his hand.

'Is that clear?' Wilder demanded, and kicked out angrily at the prone man's hip.

'All right!' Craven yelled. 'All right. You're the boss. Now leave me alone, will you? Just leave me alone.'

At a signal from Wilder, Rey released his weight from Craven's hand, allowing the younger gunman to pull himself into a sitting position and nurse his bruised fingers.

The sound of footsteps on the gravel path outside the window startled them all. Wilder pressed his back against the wall, crouched, and lifted a corner of the curtain so that he could see outside. He made agitated gestures at the other two men to keep Lancing and the women quiet. The footsteps were loud and heavy, obviously those of a man.

Obeying Wilder's signals, Rey helped Lancing from his chair and ushered him across the room. He was made to crouch so close to the gunman that the shotgun rested against his cheek and the herby smell of shampoo reached his nostrils. When he peered through the glass, he saw a tall, broad-shouldered man in his early twenties, with a healthy, weather-beaten face and hands which carried the marks of hard manual labour.

'Who is he?' Wilder demanded in a whisper.

'I don't know!'

'Then what the hell is he doing here?'

'I think I can explain that,' Catherine said. She rose to her feet and walked to the window, where she looked carefully at the young man who was now crouching in the driveway, staring at a section of the lawn.

'He's a gardener,' she said. 'He's come to inspect the borders, to see what work needs to be done.'

'Will he come to the house?' Wilder was scowling.

Lancing was disappointed when Catherine shook her head. He could have used an extra man on his side.

'How long will he be here?'

'Not long. He can't start work until next week-end. He's only looking around.'

Wilder seemed suspicious. He ducked back when the young man stood up and turned his face towards the house.

'He can't see us,' Catherine assured him. 'The curtains are too heavy. Don't worry about him. Just give him a few minutes to look over the grounds, and he'll be on his way.'

Wilder waved Lancing and Catherine back to their seats, then hurried quietly from room to room, trying to keep the gardener in his sights. He was part of the way down the hall, waiting tensely, when the doorbell rang.

'I thought you said he wouldn't come to the house?' Craven leaned over the back of the sofa and spoke harshly to Catherine. She turned her face away, offended by his unpleasant breath. When he could provoke no response from her, he turned his attention to Shirley, who shrank back as he began to stroke her hair.

The doorbell rang a second time.

Kevin Rey moved silently from the room to stand beside Wilder in the hall.

After a long interval, the footsteps descended the steps, passed under the kitchen window, and headed for the side of the house. Without making a sound, Rey hurried down the short hall to make sure that the side door was secured. No sooner had he checked the bolts than the knob turned in the gardener's hand and the door rattled slightly against its locks. The heavy rapping which followed seemed to echo round the house.

Alone in the sitting-room with the three captives, Joe Craven was holding his pistol against Shirley's neck, unaware that it had been emptied of its ammunition. With his free hand, he caressed her cheek and throat, each stroke taking his fingers closer to the deep neckline of her jacket. She whimpered softly, her eyes tightly closed and body rigid. From where she was sitting, Catherine Lancing could have reached out and pulled the big knife from his belt.

Lancing licked the dryness from his lips. Perhaps he had

been cooped up with the gang for too long, perhaps he was no longer capable of laying his life on the line for nothing stronger than a probability. Whatever the reasons, he suddenly felt that he was not made of the stuff of heroes, after all. When he tried to imagine Catherine grabbing the knife and plunging it into Craven's back, he knew that he would not be able to rely on his own instincts to follow up the move.

Outside, the gardener strode round the house and headed towards the garage. The heavy doors swung open and, once inside, the footsteps could not be heard from the house. Wilder and Rey both watched the man from upper windows. Their constant vigilance made Lancing wonder if they would shoot, if they considered it necessary.

Craven's grubby hand dipped inside Shirley's jacket. She gasped and tried to pull away from him, but he silenced and subdued her in one movement by pressing the side of his pistol across her throat from behind. The instant she stopped struggling, he released the pressure on her windpipe, allowing her to breathe more easily. When his rough handling of her breasts caused her to renew her struggles, he merely tightened his grip until she was forced into submission.

Lancing felt himself shudder on Shirley's behalf. Thinking of her with Wilder had been no more distressing than the jealousy he felt in knowing that she was capable of making love to a man other than himself, but Craven was different. Craven was little more than an animal. It was unthinkable that such a person should put his hands on Shirley.

Lancing closed his eyes for a moment and tried to shake off that extra painful sensation that Craven's behaviour caused him to feel. Shirley represented his personal life, his very private happiness, and it was humiliating to have Craven sully it by degrading her. He wanted to protect her, not only for his own sake, but for her own.

Kevin Rey came back into the room so quietly that Craven was unaware of his presence until he was standing close behind him. He released Shirley with a start, then moved quickly away from the sofa, his laughter nervous and high-pitched.

'He's still out there, nosing about in the garage,' Wilder said, entering the room. 'Keep your voices down, and stay away from the windows until he's gone.'

Lancing breathed a sigh of relief. The threat of having to perform some action which might prove to be beyond his capabilities had brought him out in a cold sweat.

'You offered me a deal,' Wilder said, watching Lancing closely from the opposite chair.

Lancing glanced at Rey and hoped that his chances, however slender, of striking up some kind of agreement with the man were not about to be blown sky-high. Rey was not a greedy man, and Lancing was sure that he would settle for much less than Wilder intended to take.

'Well?'

Lancing nodded his agreement.

'The problem is, you don't have very much to offer, do you?'

'Fifty-fifty,' Lancing said. 'You take half.'

'Half of what?'

'Half the contents of the vault,' Lancing said, guardedly.

The other man smiled, warmly and intimately.

'And what, I wonder, does that add up to in terms of hard cash?'

Lancing was silent, reluctant to speak in front of Rey, and careful not to offer any more information than Wilder already had. At the same time, he was hoping that Rey would consider taking over leadership, and accepting the deal for himself.

The gunman sat back in the velvet-covered chair, clasped his hands behind his head and crossed one leg over the other. His dark eyes sparkled and his mouth stretched into a wide grin as he displayed all the signs of a man who was much entertained by his own private thoughts.

'Would you offer me the girl?' he suddenly asked.

'What?'

'A simple enough question, Mr Lancing. Would you throw in your mistress as part of the deal?'

Lancing looked at Shirley. Her eyes were wide and frightened, and her face drained of colour. Like him, she could not be sure of the exact meaning behind Wilder's words.

'Throw in the girl, and I might be interested, but without her, we don't even discuss it. What do you say?'

Thoughts raced through Lancing's mind. Wilder didn't need his consent, so what the hell was he working up to? Did he intend taking Shirley with him when the job was finished? Was she to be shared amongst them all? Was she to be killed?

'What do you intend . . .'

'No questions,' Wilder interrupted. 'Just a straight answer. Yes or no. What's it to be?'

Shirley was shaking her head slowly from side to side, a look of real fear on her face. He avoided looking at Catherine, and he ignored Craven's sneering laughter. He had no choice. If baiting him amused Wilder, there was nothing he could do but play along with the game.

'All right,' he whispered.

'I'm sorry, what was that? Did you speak?'

'I said, all right,' Lancing repeated, meeting Wilder's gaze with what he hoped was the right amount of resistance. 'Take her. She's yours.'

'Sensible man,' Wilder nodded. 'Now we're starting to understand each other. There's just one small detail. She's not exactly mine. You see, we have to be fair about this. Like Craven said, it's *his* turn.'

A small cry escaped Shirley's lips, and Lancing felt sick and cold somewhere in the pit of his stomach.

'Is it still all right, Mr Lancing?' Wilder sneered.

There was no way that Lancing could protect Shirley from any member of the gang, yet still he felt that his words would condemn her to the worst kind of degradation. Watching Wilder's face, he knew that his discomfort was all part of the sport, and exactly what the gunman had anticipated.

'Yes,' he said hoarsely. 'It's still all right.'

thirteen

The garage doors were slammed closed and the heavy footsteps headed back towards the house.

Wilder leaped to his feet and dashed back to the window, cursing under his breath as the gardener came back into view. The man was singing to himself in a deep, strong voice as he paused close to the window. The sound of his footsteps became indistinct, as if he was standing in one place and moving his feet only slightly as he surveyed his surroundings. His outline was clearly visible as he inspected the flower beds directly outside the window. He was whistling, now, blissfully unaware of the shotgun aimed at his back.

Shirley Foster's hands came slowly to her face to cover her mouth and nose. Above her painted fingernails, her eyes were bigger and bluer than Lancing had ever seen them before. The expression he saw in them made him ache with pity for her. She was staring at the window, her body tense, her breathing rapid and shallow. Lancing fancied that he knew exactly what was on her mind. Faced with the prospect of being handed over to Joe Craven, she was allowing her hysteria to take over. She had no reason to consider Lancing's fate, nor Catherine's, nor even the safety of the unfortunate gardener. She wanted out. The look on her face said it all. *Anything* was preferable to what was in store for her.

'No, Shirley . . . Look out . . . she's going to scream . . .'

Lancing's warning was aimed at Kevin Rey, who was standing just to the right of his chair. The big man moved quickly, and grabbed Shirley by the throat to stifle the scream which was already on her lips.

The whistling outside the window stopped abruptly. The gardener tilted his head, listening, and it seemed that he looked straight into the barrel of the shotgun through the heavy lace curtains.

Rey made a hissing noise through his teeth to attract Wilder's attention. While Shirley struggled to draw breath past the pressure of his hand, he tossed his own pistol across to his boss. Fitted with a silencer, it was more suitable than the shotgun for use in a quiet suburb.

He transferred his grip from Shirley's throat to her mouth, allowing her to breathe only through her nose. Her struggles ceased and her nostrils became pinched as she tried to draw enough breath through them to feed her lungs. His free hand patted her shoulder, perhaps unconsciously, as he watched the man outside the window. In spite of the circumstances, his facial expression registered no emotion whatsoever.

Craven dipped his hands into the pockets of Lancing's jacket, found a large handkerchief and folded it diagonally into a long strip. With Rey's help, he then used it to gag Shirley, making sure that her mouth was closed and her lips stretched across her teeth before pulling the knots as tight as he could. He retied her hands behind her back to prevent her removing the gag, then stood behind her, looking down at the area of pale thigh above her stocking tops, which had become exposed in her struggles with Rey.

The man outside resumed his cheerful whistling, no doubt convinced that he had not, after all, heard sounds from inside the house. He began to move away, but had taken no more than three strides when the telephone rang.

Catherine Lancing's hand shot out and grabbed the receiver at the first ring. She let out her breath with a shuddering sigh as the uninterrupted whistling receded, along with the footsteps, towards the front of the house.

There was a flurry of almost silent activity in the room. Craven was waved to one of the windows which overlooked the front of the house, so that he could watch the gardener's movements. Wilder tossed the pistol back to Rey, who caught it easily and held it against Catherine's head. Then the gang leader perched elegantly on the arm of Lancing's chair and waited.

'Is that you, George?' Catherine's voice was almost normal. 'Yes, I'm fine, thank you. No, Max didn't manage his weekend trip . . . something came up . . . something he needs to talk to you about . . .'

102

Wilder made impatient gestures with his fingers.

'If you'll hold on, George,' Catherine said, 'I'll get Max to the phone.'

Wilder took the receiver and held it at arm's length.

'Make it sound good,' he whispered to Lancing. 'Get him here with that key as quickly as possible, but if he so much as suspects that anything's wrong . . .'

He let the threat hang in the air, unfinished, but effective. Then he held the receiver against Lancing's ear and leaned forward so that their heads were almost touching as he strained to hear both sides of the conversation.

'George, is that you?' Lancing's voice was much steadier than he had expected it to be.

'Yes, Max, what's the trouble?'

'A mix-up over one of the orders. One of the *special* orders.'

'But how? I don't understand.'

'I can't explain the details over the phone,' Lancing said. He could imagine his portly, cautious partner frowning and drumming his fingers on the nearest flat surface.

'So, what do you want me to do?'

'Just get here as fast as you can with the other vault key, and let's get our heads together to sort this mess out.'

'Can't it wait until tomorrow?'

'No, it can't,' Lancing said, surprised at the ease with which the conversation was progressing. 'Unless I can sort this matter out in the next couple of hours, we're going to be set back five, maybe even ten years.'

'That bad?'

'That bad,' Lancing confirmed. It was like eavesdropping on somebody else's conversation.

'Give me an hour, then,' Warwick said, his voice brisk and businesslike.

'Make it fifty minutes?'

Warwick snorted good-naturedly. He took his partner's words to be a quip about his careful driving.

'I'll see you in an hour, Max,' he repeated, and hung up without waiting for a reply.

Lancing turned his head as the receiver was replaced on its

cradle. George Warwick was not going to like what was happening. He was a hard-working man who wouldn't take kindly to being on the losing end of a robbery. He was touchy, with definite views on the rights and freedom of the individual. He just might manage to tip the scales enough to give Lancing room to manoeuvre if both men acted calmly, because the ever cautious senior partner kept a fully loaded pistol next to the cash box.

'You did all right,' Wilder said.

Lancing nodded and rested his shoulders against the back of his chair. He was troubled by a strong desire to urinate, which was making him feel uncomfortable.

Joe Craven came back into the room with a smile on his face.

'The gardener's gone,' he said. 'Took his time in getting off the premises, but he's gone. Who's got some smokes?'

He rummaged in the drawers of Lancing's desk and found a packet containing two slim cigars. He lit one and sucked smoke deep into his lungs, coughing as the strong tobacco burned his throat. He had removed his socks, revealing areas of dirt between his toes and round his ankles. His belt was unfastened, the zipper on his denims only partly closed. He offered Wilder the second cigar, and looked disappointed when he did not accept it. Then he leaned forward and whispered something which the others could not hear.

'You'd better ask Lancing,' Wilder said. The glint of amusement was back in his eyes, and the smile which lifted only one corner of his mouth was cruel.

Craven shuffled across the carpet and bobbed his head in a series of mock bows before Lancing. He was grinning as he held out his hands in a gesture of prayer.

'Ask him,' Wilder urged. 'Go on, ask the man.'

'Please, sir,' Craven mocked, thoroughly enjoying the game. 'Please can I screw your woman?'

Shirley struggled against her bonds, making guttural noises behind the tight gag. She would know, as Lancing knew, that to deny the gunman's request would not guarantee her safety.

'Yes.' Lancing's voice was little more than a strained whisper.

'Beg your pardon, sir?' Craven cupped his fingers behind one ear and screwed up his face. 'Can't hear you, sir. What's that you say?'

'Yes,' Lancing repeated.

'I can screw your woman? Really?'

'Yes,' Lancing said again.

Craven glanced at Wilder, who nodded his head without taking his eyes from Lancing's face. Then he pulled Shirley roughly to her feet and shoved her towards the door.

Lancing closed his eyes and tried not to listen to the sounds of her panic as Shirley was dragged upstairs to the bedroom. His teeth clenched so tightly that his jaws ached, and he could feel the veins standing out in his face and neck. His skin was hot, sweat stood out on his forehead, and his heart pounded against his chest. What he experienced was agonizing and exhausting, a spasm which wracked his body with unfamiliar strength. It was like a silent scream.

'You're a bastard, Wilder.' Kevin Rey spoke quietly, with no hint of accusation in his voice. He was merely stating a fact which he believed to be obvious.

'Does that mean you disapprove of my methods?' Wilder asked.

'Not really. I think it's your motives I don't like.'

'And what would you, or anyone else for that matter, know about my motives?'

Rey shrugged his broad shoulders and settled himself comfortably in an armchair.

'Shall I tell you what I think?' he offered, amiably.

'By all means.'

'I think you're after two things.' He held up two fingers and tapped one of them with the end of his pistol. 'One: for private reasons, you want to break Lancing. You want to put him down, ruin his business, take his money and his easy life away from him. Right?'

'Go on,' Wilder said, admitting nothing.

Rey tapped the end of his second finger. Sounds from the bedroom above his head distracted him for no more than a few seconds.

'Two: a good businessman keeps books, and our shopkeeper is a damn good businessman, so he probably has records of all his deals. The shop's a cover for something illegal, I've gathered that much. Lancing's pretty well known as a speculator in diamonds, so I reckon he could name some of the big men who do the buying, selling, and transporting of stones that are ... stolen? ... smuggled? ...'

Wilder spat out the matchstick which he had chewed to a pulp, then used a toothpick to scrape bits of softened wood from between his teeth.

'What I think you're *really* after,' Rey continued, 'is a list of those names. Once you have them, you could make a bundle out of blackmail, take-overs, raids, anything you have a taste for. Either way, Lancing's the whipping boy, because someone, somewhere, is going to work out just where you got all your information from. You've got the poor bastard by the short and curlies from the minute you open that vault.'

'Very clever,' Wilder conceded. 'But aren't you forgetting one important detail?'

'What's that?'

'Well, this isn't my job, remember?'

'Ah, yes.' Rey's smile broadened. 'The syndicate. Your trump card, eh, Wilder?'

Wilder nodded, his eyes creased by his broad smile.

'My trump card,' he said.

'Or your bluff,' Rey countered.

Wilder's smile did not falter, but the amusement faded from his eyes as he held Rey's steady, noncommittal stare. If he was trying to read the other man's face, he was getting nowhere.

'Hey, I just thought of something else,' Rey said, after a lengthy pause.

'Well?'

'After the robbery, the newspapers make a big splash of the whole thing. Lancing's off the hook, his partner and his women are all off his back, and you *both* collect. Anyway, it makes no difference to me.'

'No?' Wilder tilted his head and raised one eyebrow.

'Not at all. The only thing I want out of this job is my fair

106

share.' He got up from the chair and gently nudged the pile of stolen items with his foot. 'I don't want to take the risk of having to fence this stuff in a hurry, and you did promise me a better deal, so I'll settle for cash. Don't get me wrong. I'm not trying to push you. All I want is a fair share, in cash, and I'm happy. I reckon I can trust you to come across with my share when the time comes. OK if I go make some fresh coffee?'

Wilder nodded. Only when Rey had left the room did he allow his smile to fade. After a small, thoughtful pause, he shrugged his shoulders and leaned forward to pick up an object which had rolled towards his foot. He held it in front of him, turning it carefully in his fingers as he admired the intricate carving on the smooth, highly-polished stone. He glanced at Lancing and smiled.

'The Queen,' he said, holding out the ornate chess piece. 'The easiest way to dethrone a King is via his Queen. She's his strength and his weakness, his closest friend and his deadliest enemy. Think of it, Lancing. I could have bribed your wife to leave the doors unbolted, so that we could sit out the hours in comfort while we waited for Warwick. I could have bribed your mistress to tell me about the vault. I could have got at you through either of your Queens . . . or both. Does the tactic sound familiar, Lancing?'

It did. Lancing had always maintained that a man's chief weakness was the woman he cared for, because she was close enough to extract his secrets and command his trust. He had sought to make himself invulnerable by never speaking about his deals to the women in his life, and never getting himself so deeply involved that he became careless. He had loved deeply and carelessly only once in his life, and that woman had almost destroyed him. He had adored her with all the passion of his eighteen years, and she had repaid him by running off with a wealthy French businessman, robbing him of his happiness and the baby daughter he idolized. He had never set eyes on them again, in spite of two long years of frantic searching, but the experience had changed his whole personality. Ironically, he had a faithless teenager and her illegitimate daughter to thank for the success he had made of his life. Remembering this, he had no doubt that Wilder was right. The best way to dethrone a King was through his Queen.

He was thankful when Rey brought the coffee, and the small exchange with Wilder was at an end. He watched Wilder drop the chess piece to the carpet so that he could concentrate on holding the cup and saucer, and was glad to be free of the veiled accusations. The image of his baby daughter was still very clear in his mind, reminding him, in turn, of the laughing little boy who had so briefly taken her place. The memories carried with them a pain which surprised him not only by its intensity, but by its very existence. He had thought himself cured of the hurt. Sixteen years was too long to mourn a son, and thirty years too long to mourn a daughter. He looked at Catherine and suddenly realized that, like him, she had borne the terrible grief of her son's death alone and uncomforted. Perhaps, deep down, they both still grieved, even after all the years of pretending that it no longer mattered.

fourteen

Wilder looked past Lancing to the door which led to the stairs. His lips tightened and his brows pulled down into a deep scowl.

'Where's the girl?' he asked, sharply.

'Sleeping it off.' Craven's reply was accompanied by a loud snigger.

'Fetch her.'

'Oh, leave her up there. She needs the rest.'

'I said, fetch her,' Wilder repeated. Without raising his voice, he conveyed both authority and impatience. 'Just a minute, Craven. What's that in your hand?'

'Hair.'

'What?'

'Soft, sweet-smelling, silky hair. Here, Lancing, recognize it?'

Lancing's flesh crawled as the handful of auburn hair was thrust into his face.

'Go get the girl, Craven.' Wilder's words were ground out through clenched teeth. He fished in his pocket until he found a fresh wooden toothpick, then turned to the window and flexed his shoulder and arm muscles as if he had backache.

Lancing stared at the back of Wilder's head and took several deep breaths. Dread made his belly taut and his scalp prickle, but he was determined to remain absolutely calm, no matter with what situation he might be faced.

Shirley Foster was guided unsteadily across the room and shoved towards the sofa, where she fell in an ungainly sprawl. Hampered by the cord which still bound her wrists behind her back, she slumped forward until her face was pushed against the upholstered arm of the sofa. She was trembling violently, and her breathing was ragged behind the gag. She was shoeless, one of her stockings was twisted out of shape and the other was torn from ankle to thigh. Her skirt was creased, her jacket gaping open where at least two more buttons had been ripped off. Barely covered by the crumpled fabric, her pale breasts bore the cruel marks of Craven's passion.

Kevin Rey stepped forward and lifted Shirley's face so that he could inspect the bruises on her cheeks and neck. His fingers were gentle as they touched the front of her head, where a large section of hair had been hacked away so close to her scalp that the skin was spotted with blood.

'She loved it.' Craven sniggered. 'Women enjoy a bit of rough handling, once in a while.'

The backward sweep of Rey's hand was unexpected and savage. His whole body arched with the swing of it, and his clenched fist connected with Craven's face with such force that he was lifted off his feet. He staggered against Lancing's chair before falling heavily to the floor, stunned.

Lancing stared at the semi-conscious man and welcomed the cold rage which stirred inside him. It worked like an anaesthetic, numbing the rawness of other emotions which had threatened to surface when he saw what had happened to Shirley. Had his hands not been tied behind his back, he could have reached down and grabbed the knife which protruded from the gunman's belt. It would have been so easy. A twist of the wrist, a blow no heavier than a punch against the soft belly, and Craven would have died there at his feet before anyone else in the room realized what was going on. At that moment Lancing chalked up another reason for getting himself free of Wilder without finishing up with a pack of vengeful ex-clients on his heels. He needed plenty of time and space if he was going to track down, and kill, Joe Craven.

Wilder was smiling. He nodded his head very slightly, but enough to show Lancing that he knew what was on his mind.

'This is unforgivable . . .' Catherine's voice was strained. She accepted a paper clip from Kevin Rey, which she used to draw the two sides of Shirley's jacket together. Then she used her handkerchief to wipe the tears from the other woman's face.

'So what do you care?' Wilder snapped. 'You don't give a shit about your husband's mistress, so don't let's have any hysterics on her behalf.'

'I care about this . . . any woman would.'

'Surely you don't feel sorry for her?' Wilder's voice was sharp with sarcasm.

'Of course I do . . .'

'Balls!' He spat the word at her. 'Revenge is sweet, isn't that what they say, Mrs Lancing? You can get satisfaction for every wrong you think she's done you, and all you have to do is sit back and watch.'

'That's not true . . .'

'Oh, yes it is, lady. You don't have to play the innocent with me. I've had you figured out right from the start, and there's not a single move in this game that you haven't wrung your little bit of pleasure from . . .' he glanced at Kevin Rey and lifted one corner of his mouth in a half-smile before adding, '. . . not *one*.'

'That's a lie. I . . .' Catherine's protests were silenced by

Craven's curses as he pulled himself to his feet and leaned against the bookshelf for support. He held one hand to the side of his face where the flesh was already beginning to swell close to his eye. There was a small trickle of blood at the side of his mouth at which he dabbed gingerly with one finger.

'I want out, Wilder,' he said, groggily. 'I've had a skinful of this set-up. Give me my half of the cash and let me get the hell out of here.'

'Stuff it, Craven. You don't go nowhere until this job's finished.'

'I want *out*,' Craven insisted. 'I've got what I came for, and I want *out*.'

'You stay.' Wilder's tone and manner were menacing.

'Oh, let him go,' Rey cut in. 'Let him move out, if he's had enough. We don't need him. There's no reason for him to hang around here.'

'Oh, yes?' Wilder removed the toothpick from his teeth and surveyed its chewed end. 'And what do we do after he's gone, sit here like prize turkeys while he blows the whistle on us?'

Rey looked at Craven and shrugged. 'All right. So he stays,' he said amiably.

'He stays,' Wilder repeated coldly.

Seething with unconcealed anger, Craven bent down to retrieve the tuft of hair which had fallen from his hand. He searched through the drawers of the desk until he found a rubber band, which he used to secure the hair at its cut end. Then he flopped down in one of the chairs and nursed his head in his hands. After a short time, he raised his head and scowled at Lancing.

'What the fuck are you gaping at?'

The question startled Lancing, who had been unaware that he was staring.

Rey and Wilder were both over by the window. Craven glanced at them before leaning forward in his seat and grinning at Lancing.

'She's a good screw,' he sneered.

Lancing ignored the taunt.

'Nice tits she's got . . .'

Lancing watched Craven lick his lips, but refused to rise to the bait.

'Maybe I'll cut the rest of her hair off, next time.' He placed the lock of hair against his face and sniffed. 'Your woman smells nice. I might have her again . . . She's a damn good screw . . .'

'You touch her again and I'll . . .' Lancing bit back the threat, furious that he had allowed the gunman to provoke him.

'You'll what, Lancing? What'll you do, huh? What'll you do to me for screwing your tart? Are you going to come after me, track me down, *kill* me?' He laughed aloud. 'Stuff you, old man. I won't be looking over my shoulder on your account. You may be a big noise in the jewellery business, but as far as I'm concerned, you're about as frightening as a used fart.'

He roared with laughter and rubbed Shirley's hair between his finger and thumb.

'Why don't you shut your mouth, Craven?' Wilder snapped. He began to pace the room restlessly, spitting out bits of wood and scowling.

'He's late.'

'No, he's not,' Rey contradicted. 'He has another five minutes yet. Give the man a chance.'

'I could have made it in half the time.'

'Sure you could, Vince. And there'd be a couple of traffic cops on your tail, just to confirm your time. Relax. He'll be here, soon.'

'I need to go to the lavatory,' Lancing blurted out suddenly. Acknowledging his need seemed to intensify his discomfort.

Rey glanced at Wilder, noted the brief nod of his head, then jerked his pistol to indicate that Lancing could leave the room. He followed close on his heels, stepping back quickly when Lancing stopped outside the downstairs lavatory door.

'What's the matter?'

'I need my hands . . . unless you want to oblige.'

Rey looked at him closely, as if trying to guess his intentions.

'Take your pick,' Lancing said, evenly. 'Untie me or unzip

112

me, but make it quick, will you? I don't think I can hold out much longer.'

One corner of Rey's mouth twitched in what was almost a smile. 'I didn't hurt her,' he said, unexpectedly. 'Your wife's a nice woman, and I never hurt women. That's not my style.'

'Thanks.' Lancing glanced back up the short hallway and lowered his voice. 'He hasn't told you everything,' he whispered.

'What do you mean?' Rey's frown narrowed his grey eyes so that he appeared to be looking at Lancing through his light-coloured lashes.

'He's selling you short.'

'You'd better not be lying, Lancing.'

'I swear I'm not . . . Wilder's selling you short . . . There's enough in that vault to . . .'

'What's going on out here?' Wilder walked into the hall from the sitting-room, his shotgun raised.

'There's nothing going on, Vince.'

'My hands,' Lancing reminded Rey in a sharp tone. He turned his back to allow the other man to unfasten the necktie which bound his wrists. His eyes met the steady stare of Wilder, who watched him with obvious suspicion. It was impossible to tell how much he might have overheard. He breathed a deep sigh of relief when he was allowed to enter the lavatory and partly close the door behind him.

Wilder almost pounced on him when he re-emerged. He was very tense.

'A car has just pulled into the drive. Go check it out.' He gave Lancing a hard shove towards the other room, then pulled him against the wall so that he could look from the window without being seen from outside.

George Warwick stepped from his car and locked the door carefully behind him. Then he smoothed his trousers, buttoned his jacket, and adjusted the near-side wing mirror before walking briskly towards the front door of the house.

'That's him,' Lancing confirmed. 'That's George Warwick.'

Wilder shoved him towards the sofa, then took Catherine

Lancing by the arm and pushed her down the hall. Craven was already standing behind the door, his pistol held in his right hand and pointing towards the ceiling as he pressed himself against the wall.

George Warwick dropped his customary, dry-lipped kiss on Catherine's left cheek. If he was surprised to find her still in her dressing-gown, neither his words nor his manner betrayed the fact. As he strode down the hall to the sitting-room, he was smiling and making small-talk about the weather, unaware that anything was wrong until he spotted Lancing and Shirley on the sofa. His smile faded and his mouth hung open. He gaped at Shirley's bruised face, the gag which cut into her skin, the dishevelled condition of her clothes. He spun on his heels, looking past Catherine to where Craven still leaned against the wall by the door, and Wilder stood just inside the kitchen doorway. He stared back into the room, at the stained carpet, the untidy pile of valuables, the big man perched on the arm of a chair with a gun in his hand.

'Oh, my God . . .'

'Take it easy, George,' Lancing said calmly.

'What *is* this? What in hell's name is going *on* here?'

Wilder's shot gun touched the fleshy part below his left ear, and a pair of glinting brown eyes met his own.

'Does this answer your question, Mr Warwick?'

'A robbery . . . ?'

'A robbery,' Wilder confirmed. 'Now, all you have to do to stay alive is play along with us. Do exactly as we tell you, and you won't get hurt. Understand?'

Warwick nodded his head. He was breathing rapidly and his face had paled.

'Take it easy, George,' Lancing repeated, remembering his partner's high blood pressure. 'There's nothing to worry about, just as long as you do as they say.'

Warwick was staring at Shirley Foster as if unable to identify the leggy, vivacious mistress of his partner with this pathetic young woman. Without otherwise acknowledging the hand on his arm, he allowed Catherine Lancing to steer him to a chair.

114

'The key,' Wilder said, snapping his fingers and holding out his hand.

Warwick looked questioningly at Lancing.

'The key,' Wilder repeated.

'There's an alarm,' Warwick protested. 'It'll trip . . . it's difficult to handle . . .'

'*The key*,' Wilder snapped, illustrating his impatience by shoving his shotgun hard against the other man's neck.

Warwick dipped into his pocket and came up with a ring containing perhaps half a dozen keys. They were immediately snatched from his hand by Craven, who began to compare them with the keys on Lancing's bunch.

'A matching pair,' he announced after a brief search. He held up two brass keys, one from each ring. He was grinning broadly, as if he considered the matching of the keys to be a matter of skill.

Warwick stared at him with the same fixed, contemptuous stare as Lancing had seen him use whenever he found himself confronted by men he considered inferior.

'Those,' he said deliberately, 'are the keys to the garage at the rear of the shop.'

Rey sniggered, and Wilder's broad grin erased some of the lines of tension from his own face. Without warning, the furious Craven hurled the keys at Warwick. Their impact left a deep scratch on his upper lip and another on the bridge of his nose.

Rey turned his back in a clear attempt to hide his amusement, but Wilder faced the younger gunman with a sarcastic grin.

'Maybe you'd like to rob the garage, instead,' he quipped. 'Maybe you think a couple of spare tyres and a bag of tools are worth more than what's in the vault, huh?'

'Get stuffed, Wilder. Anyone can make a mistake.'

'Yes, yes, of course.' Wilder's grin widened. He held out his hand for the twin keys which Warwick had separated from the others on the bunch. 'Thank you, Mr Warwick. I'm glad to see that *somebody* around here knows what he's doing.'

115

Warwick made no answer. He was wary of the friction which he sensed between the two men. A droplet of blood had oozed from the scratch and slid down to hang from the end of his nose. He wiped it away with a neatly folded handkerchief.

Joe Craven had crossed to the window, where he stood scowling and biting his nails sulkily. He turned at the sound of Warwick's cigarette lighter.

'Hey, old man,' he snarled. 'Didn't anyone ever tell you it's fucking bad manners to smoke all by yourself?' He strode back to Warwick's chair and snatched both packet and lighter from his hand. Then he took the lighted cigarette from his mouth and dropped it to the carpet.

'Step on it,' he ordered.

Warwick was breathing heavily, but his gaze was steady as he looked up at the gunman. Instead of obeying the order, he stooped to retrieve his cigarette. He winced, but made no sound when Craven stamped on his hand.

'I said, step on it, old man.'

Lancing saw the glance which passed between Wilder and Rey. He wondered if the gang leader's policy was to allow Craven enough rein to satisfy his sadistic nature *and* intimidate his prisoners.

'*Do it!*' Craven yelled, grinding his heel on Warwick's bent fingers.

Warwick's face contorted in pain, but he didn't cry out. When the pressure on his fingers eased, he drew back his hand and crushed the cigarette beneath his shoe.

Craven swaggered away, satisfied to have had the last word. He lit one of the cigarettes and stuffed the rest into the pocket of his denims. He drew deeply and slowly, filling his lungs with smoke and then blowing it from his nostrils in twin streams.

Sitting on the sofa between Catherine and Shirley, Lancing held his hands behind his back and hoped that nobody would notice that his wrists had been left untied. He tried to hear the whispered conversation which was going on between Rey and Wilder.

'I just want to make sure,' Rey was saying.

'You mean you don't trust me?'

116

'Why the hell should I?'

Wilder flicked the end of his matchstick with his tongue. 'There's no other way we can work it out,' he said. 'Lancing and Warwick have to be the ones who handle the vault. We can't risk tripping the alarm, and I can't let myself in and out of that shop in broad daylight without them to make it look good. You could always come with us, and leave Craven here with the women.'

'He'll have us all on a damn murder charge if we leave him in charge here,' Rey snorted quietly. 'But tell me, Wilder, what's to stop you hot-arsing it away with whatever it is you came for, and leaving me here to explain to the cops?'

'You have my word,' Wilder assured him coolly.

Rey lifted one eyebrow and tilted his face to one side. He made clicking noises with his tongue as he stretched his lips into a friendly smile.

'Convince me,' he said. 'Convince me that you don't intend working the classic double-cross, with me on the losing end.'

'How?'

'Leave me your passport.'

Wilder hesitated only briefly before reaching into his inside pocket and handing his passport over.

'And something else, Wilder.'

'What?'

'Leave me the shotgun . . . With one clear set of your finger-prints on it.'

'Like hell, I will.' Wilder was still smiling, but a brittle note had crept into his voice.

Rey shrugged his shoulders and stared back at Wilder, who made the first move. Slowly, he removed one of his gloves, picked up the shotgun and aimed it at Rey. Then he placed it carefully across a corner of the trolley and replaced his glove.

'Satisfied, Kevin?' he asked.

'Satisfied,' Rey nodded, smiling.

Observing them from his cramped position on the sofa, Lancing noted every detail of the scene. Rey's show of deter-mination had been both discreet and firm. He had questioned Wilder, shown mistrust of him, refusing simply to fall in with

117

his plans, yet at no time had he appeared to offer an open challenge. Rey was looking for equality rather than the upper hand, but any move he made against Wilder's leadership could only benefit Lancing.

fifteen

As Vince Wilder gave final instructions to his men, it occurred to Lancing that the basement of his own shop might offer him his last chance of staying alive. In exchange for the incriminating shotgun, Rey had handed over the pistol with the silencer, so, once the vault was open, there was nothing to stop Wilder killing both partners before making his getaway. The loaded gun in the vault would only be really useful if Lancing could get to it first. Warwick would be neither fast enough nor ruthless enough to use it, and besides, he would probably go for Craven first, not knowing that the man's gun was empty. Walking into that basement would be like walking into a sealed trap, with no escape if something prevented him getting at the pistol in the vault. Just thinking about it made him feel concerned.

'We'll take that car,' Wilder said, pointing through the window at the dark green coupé standing in the drive. 'You can take the wheel, Lancing, and Warwick can sit beside you. Craven and I will be in the back, so don't try anything stupid.'

'You intend to kill me, don't you?' Lancing blurted out on impulse. 'As soon as you get what's in the vault, you intend to kill me. Isn't that right?'

'Just keep your mouth shut and don't push me.'

'But I'm right, aren't I?' Lancing insisted. He wanted to plant doubts in Rey's mind, so that the man would know exactly what he might be involved with. He ignored Wilder's icy stare.

118

'You do intend to kill me, don't you?'

'Shut your mouth, Lancing.'

'Open vault . . . bullet in head . . . all neat and tidy,' Lancing persisted. He smiled with difficulty. It was all too near the possible truth for his liking.

Wilder adjusted the silencer on the pistol. 'There are more ways to kill a man than by putting a bullet in his head,' he said, with exaggerated patience.

'I'm glad to hear that, Vince.' Rey's voice was steady. 'You've absolutely nothing to worry about, Mr Shopkeeper. There'll be no killing on this job. Isn't that right, Vince?'

For Rey's benefit, Lancing allowed his relief to show. So long as Rey held the passport and the gun with the fingerprints, Wilder was unlikely to risk pushing him into a panic move.

Lancing drove slowly down the driveway and out into the tree-lined avenue. The neighbourhood was quiet, bathed in sunshine and rich in the smells of grass and flowers. He could hear children's laughter coming from the sprawling, single-storey house across the way, and he glimpsed a crimson swimsuit between the trees as a slender young woman dived into the pool beyond. It was a typical, warm Sunday morning, with nothing to shatter the quiet but the buzz of a lawnmower or the thwack of a tennis ball against a racket. Lancing shuddered as he wound up the window against the sounds of normality. He raised his hand and smiled at the man who walked his two dogs along the avenue at a leisurely pace. A portly, middle-aged man, he tipped his hat politely as the car went by. He was not the sort of man who would pay much attention to the faces of the passengers.

Lancing stopped smoothly at the end of the avenue and waited for a slow-moving patrol car to pass before pulling out into the main road. A suntanned face scrutinized the car, but nothing about it registered as out of the ordinary to the officer behind the wheel. Lancing wondered what the man would feel like later, when it was revealed that he had come so close to a pair of armed men engaged in a robbery.

They drew up outside the shop, but remained in the car for several minutes to allow the street to clear of people. A teen-aged couple were involved in a heated argument outside the furniture shop on the corner, while an elderly man with a limp was making slow progress towards them from the other end of the street.

'Right,' Wilder said at last. 'Make it slow, but casual. Oh, and Lancing . . .' he smiled menacingly, '. . . if any of those alarms go off, the first bullet will be for you.'

The interior of the shop seemed unfamiliar, with its empty shelves and display cases. Lancing found himself looking into the corner where Craven had urinated on the carpet. The dark stain was easy to see in the sunlight which streamed in between the blinds.

With the door safely locked behind them, they went directly to the basement, where Wilder stood before the vault, licking his lips thoughtfully.

Lancing watched the gunman's face, made gaunt in the shadows cast by the single electric light bulb in the centre of the ceiling. A pulse throbbed at the side of his neck, and his dark eyes were narrowed. He worked his jaw rapidly until a well-chewed matchstick eased its way out between his teeth. He glanced at Craven, his frown deepening. It became clear to Lancing why he was hanging about instead of getting on with the job. It would drastically change the size of Wilder's profit if Craven got a look inside the vault and realized just how much cash he should have been entitled to.

'How did they know?' George Warwick asked. There was a pained expression on his face as he stared at the vault. 'Who told them? How did they find out about this?'

Lancing tensed. 'They just came in off the street and started to clean us out, George,' he said carefully.

'But they couldn't have known about all this unless some-body *told* them.'

'Shut up,' Wilder warned, his voice heavy with implied threat.

'Who told you?' Warwick insisted. 'I demand to know who

120

did this. Was it one of the customers? One of the clients? Who told you about the money and the . ..'

He doubled up and fell to his knees, clutching his belly and gasping for breath, knocked almost senseless by the impact of the handle of Craven's pistol against his soft flesh.

'Do as you're told when Mr Wilder speaks to you,' Craven sneered.

'When I want your help, I'll ask for it, Craven.'

'Yes, Mr Wilder, sir.' Craven made a mock salute, then stood back with a smile on his face to admire his handiwork.

Lancing stiffened, hesitating between going to the assistance of his partner and staying out of trouble. He decided on the latter. He was well aware how hard the situation was for Warwick. His whole future was tied up in the vault: in the shipment, the cash, and the continued goodwill of certain clients. It was Lancing's guess that one of those clients was trying to move in and take over. Wilder's vague references to syndicate connections were probably nothing more than bluff to keep the others in line. His boss had to be somebody who knew enough about the set-up to realize that robbery would be worthwhile, but not enough to be prepared for the time-lock and the twin-key system. It had to be someone who was willing to trust the job to men like Wilder, Rey and Craven, who were less than a professional team.

'What's the hold up?' Craven asked. He nudged Warwick with his foot. 'Hey, is this guy all right?'

'He'd better be,' Wilder said. 'I need him to open this door. Get him on his feet.'

'Maybe I shouldn't have hit him so hard. He sounds to be in bad shape.'

'Just get him on his feet, Craven.'

George Warwick was breathing as if something tight had been placed across his throat. His mouth was wide open, his eyes streaming, his throat rasping with every laboured breath he took. He pulled at his necktie and the collar of his shirt, but this brought no ease, and the guttural noises continued to come from his throat. His fleshy face was wet with sweat, the normally pale skin a rapidly deepening shade of purple. He pulled a small plastic container from his pocket and pushed one end of it into his mouth, sucking desperately at its contents. As Craven yanked him to his feet, the container slipped from his fingers and was crushed beneath his shoe.

Wilder drew Lancing on one side, leaving the younger gunman to support Warwick's heavy body.

'Can we open it without his help, if I follow your instructions?'

Lancing nodded his head, only half listening to Wilder's voice. He was beginning to feel concerned about the still gasping George Warwick. The crushed, unidentifiable container puzzled him. He had not been aware of his partner's need for any kind of breathing aid.

'Get moving, Lancing.'

He jerked his attention back to Wilder, who was standing before the vault door with one of the keys in his hand. The man obviously intended getting the job over while Craven was otherwise occupied, a plan which caused Lancing to tremble with anticipation. It would be him against Wilder. If he could swing the metal door between them, it would protect him from Wilder's bullets just long enough for him to grab the gun. It would be lying there, fully loaded and ready to fire, on the centre shelf next to the diamonds. He should be able to put his hand right on it at the first attempt, even in the darkness.

Following Lancing's instructions, Wilder inserted one of the small keys in the left-hand lock and turned it very carefully in an anti-clockwise direction. The mechanism clicked softly, then the light on the dial went out and the rhythmic ticking of the clock came to an abrupt halt.

'Give me the big key,' Lancing said. 'We've taken care of the time-lock, now all we have to do is get the door open without triggering the secondary alarm.'

He slid the long brass key into the lock and eased it through the sequence of turns and half-turns which would release the heavy door. Even without the time-lock to hamper him, Wilder would have been unable to open the door unaided. The complicated action of the main lock was designed for maximum security, and while it locked on contact, it could only be

opened by proper use of the release sequence. Lancing lifted
the bar which held the door in place, and withdrew the key. It
slipped from his grip and fell to the floor with a metallic ring.
For a moment he was tempted to nudge it into the vault with
his foot and slam the door, but a sideways glance at Vince
Wilder told him that such action would be foolhardy. The
pistol in the gunman's hand made a small clicking noise, as if
he sensed the reason for Lancing's hesitation. That steady,
determined finger on the trigger of a loaded gun was all Lancing needed to remind him of the danger he was facing. His
precious haul was of no use to him if he got himself killed trying to protect it.

Perspiration dampened his forehead and the palms of his
hands. He heard Craven curse as he struggled to support the
weight of George Warwick, whose breathing, if anything, had
worsened. He took a deep breath and braced his body before
pulling on the door with both hands.

Wilder's foot jammed unexpectedly against the big door as it
started to swing out from the wall. He waved the pistol at
Lancing.

Lancing backed away as the gunman pulled open the draw-
string top of the canvas bag which he had brought with him on
the raid. As the door of the vault opened a little more, he
glimpsed the shallow metal shelves with their sparse but very
valuable hoard. The single light bulb was inefficient against the
piles of boxes and old packing cases, and the shadows cast by
the partly opened door left the interior of the vault in near
darkness. He realized that the small, leather-bound book which
contained such damning details of his activities might go un-
noticed among the shadows. He could afford to let Wilder get
away with everything else, then perhaps enlist the help of some
of the more powerful men named in the book in tracking down
the gang. With the shelves almost completely hidden from his
view by the door and the gunman's body, he could only hope
that Wilder's greed would lead him straight to the bulkier,
more obviously valuable items. Over half a million in cash
and uncut diamonds must seem far more attractive than a
simple little notebook.

Wilder groped inside the vault, then smiled broadly as he withdrew his hand. The pistol he held was small and light, so that the attached silencer gave it a clumsy, unbalanced appearance. He pointed it at Lancing, and the expression on his face said that he had expected to find it there.

'I suppose it's loaded?'

Lancing nodded miserably.

'Nice try.' Wilder grinned, then waved the pistol to indicate that Lancing was to move over to where Craven still guarded the senior partner. With a safe distance between them, he proceeded to take what he wanted from the darkened interior of the vault.

George Warwick had slumped against the wall with one hand resting on a packing case in order to keep himself reasonably upright. He seemed to be using all his strength just to draw small amounts of air into his lungs and blow them out again. His skin was discoloured and his hair shiny with perspiration. As Lancing came close to him, he grabbed his wrist and held on to it with a surprisingly strong grip, staring at his partner through bulging, frightened eyes.

'What's the matter with him?' Craven asked, more interested in Warwick's condition than in what Wilder was doing.

'I don't know,' Lancing admitted.

'He can't breathe. I only hit him once, so how come the old fool can't breathe?'

'How the hell do I know?' Lancing snapped. 'Maybe you shouldn't have hit the poor bastard so hard.'

He eased Warwick towards a large wooden packing case and sat him down with his back against the wall. The heat of his body could be felt through his clothes, and his jacket and shirt were already stained with sweat. Lancing unfastened his belt and the button on the waistband of his trousers, but the asthmatic breathing continued without respite.

'What is it, George? What the hell's wrong with you? What can I do?'

Warwick stretched out a trembling arm, his bulging eyes staring at the area of floor indicated by his finger. The shattered pieces of his inhaler had been scattered underfoot.

Lancing could only hope that his life didn't depend on the substance it had once contained.

Wilder was still checking the vault shelves when the sound of some kind of disturbance reached them from the street. The breaking of a window, accompanied by jeers and catcalls, resulted in a stream of abuse from a foreign woman with a high-pitched voice. She lapsed into her native tongue as her excitement increased, punctuating her rapid babble with easily recognizable oaths.

'Upstairs,' Wilder ordered. 'No, not you, Craven. You stay here with Warwick while I find out what the hell's going on out there. Try to keep him quiet, will you? Those airvents are small, but they just might carry the sound of voices up to street level. I'll call you when we're ready to move.'

Craven shrugged his shoulders and nodded his head. His attention was riveted on Warwick's rasping attempts to breathe.

Lancing hurried obediently up the stairs, the barrel of Wilder's pistol nudging the small of his back at intervals to encourage him to keep moving. Once inside the shop, he was made to stand facing the wall with his hands above his head while Wilder crossed to the main window and peered through gaps in the blinds.

Lancing didn't need to see out in order to know what was going on. He could hear the voices of a group of youngsters who were baiting the owners of the restaurant across the street. They were too far away to draw attention to the shop, or to present any real threat to Wilder's plans, but it was doubtful if he would risk leaving the premises while there were so many people in the street. He shifted his weight from one foot to the other. The awkward position of his arms was doing much to aggravate the stiffness in his shoulders and neck. Slowly, he lowered one arm so that he could see his wristwatch, and when this small movement aroused no comment from Wilder, he brought both arms down and folded them across his chest. The new position was much easier, bringing instant relief to the bruised area at the base of his neck. He thought he heard a familiar click from the basement and guessed that Craven had just closed the vault door. No doubt the gunman had first searched the shelves for anything of value which Wilder might have overlooked.

The commotion in the street seemed to increase in intensity only seconds before a fast-moving vehicle rounded the corner with a screech of tyres and sped past the shop. Footsteps came from all directions at once as the trouble makers scattered, leaving the now sobbing foreign woman to make a loud, garbled report of the disturbance. The glass from the broken window was already being swept along the pavement and eased into safe pile by the rhythmic strokes of a broom.

'Now we wait for the street to clear,' Wilder said softly, as if talking to himself. He remained at the window, his canvas bag at his feet and his pistol ready to fire if necessary.

'How's it going, Vince?' Craven suddenly swaggered from the back room.

'Keep your voice down, you fool. I thought I told you to stay downstairs with Warwick?'

'He's quiet enough,' Craven said. 'He won't give us any trouble.'

He moved to the window and looked out, only mildly interested in what was going on in the street.

'We'll wait another ten minutes, just to make sure we're not seen leaving,' Wilder said. 'There's no sense in taking unnecessary chances.'

'You're the boss, Vince.' Craven grinned.

When Lancing looked at his watch again, the street had been quiet for some time. He assumed that they would soon be leaving the premises. His failure to get the gun from the vault had already ceased to trouble him. He still had a chance to get at Wilder through Rey, and the last fifteen minutes had given him an opportunity to work out at least the framework of a plan which might interest Wilder if all else failed. Until he could discover exactly what the gang leader had taken from the vault, however, he was unwilling to show his hand.

'Right,' Wilder said, at last. 'Go down and get the old man, and let's get out of here.'

Craven went back to the basement, only to return some time later with a sheepish grin on his face.

'I can't get the door open,' he said.

'What door?'

'The vault door. Warwick was making too much noise, so I shut him in there to keep him quiet, and now I can't get the door open.'

'You did *what*?' Wilder turned to face Craven, his expression one of absolute disbelief. 'When, for God's sake? How long has the poor bastard been in there?'

Craven shrugged his shoulders, unconcerned. 'Oh, about ten minutes, maybe fifteen.'

'You idiot. You stupid, senseless idiot.'

Lancing felt his skin crawl. The vault was tall and wide, but not deep. Warwick's overweight body would be rammed against the metal shelves, with no room to move in the confined space. It would be dark in there, a place of unimaginable horror for a man already having difficulty with his breathing.

Wilder shoved Lancing ahead of him through the back room to the basement.

'Get him out of there,' he ordered, grinding his teeth as he spoke. 'Come on, *move*. Get him out of there.'

Lancing dropped into a squat and ran his hands over the floor in front of the vault.

'I dropped the key . . . It should be right here . . .'

'Find it,' Wilder barked.

'It's gone. It isn't here.'

Wilder prodded Lancing's shoulder with his pistol.

'Find that damn key,' he repeated.

Lancing's fingers probed the dusty cracks around the vault, finding nothing. After several minutes of futile search he stood up and shook his head grimly.

'It was right here,' he said. 'It must have been kicked inside the vault when the door was open. Maybe Warwick himself . . .'

Wilder spat a sliver of wood from his mouth and scowled back at Lancing.

'How in hell do we get him out?' he asked.

'We don't, Wilder. That's a self-locking door, and Warwick has the only other key.'

'What's the difference, anyway?' Craven snapped.

Wilder's reply was a back-handed blow to the mouth which sent the younger man reeling. He staggered against a packing case and pressed his fingers to the small cut which had appeared on his lower lip. He glared briefly at Wilder before moving to the staircase, where he leaned against the wooden banister with his face set in a sullen expression.

Lancing stared at the door of the vault and tried to imagine how his partner had felt as it slammed behind him. He shuddered, sickened by his own thoughts. Even in his semi-collapsed state, George Warwick would have remembered that the vault was airtight.

sixteen

The journey back to Lancing's house was made in almost complete silence. Craven sat in the front passenger seat with his elbow propped against the door frame in order to chew his thumbnail in comfort. From time to time, he spat particles of nail from his mouth. He sniffed noisily and regularly, as if he needed to blow his nose but had no handkerchief available for the purpose.

In the rear seat, Vince Wilder seemed relaxed, outwardly unaffected by the seriousness of recent events. It was as difficult to judge his feelings as to guess what was in the canvas bag on the seat beside him.

Driving slowly, and making a conscious effort to ignore Craven's sniffing, Lancing took stock of the new position in which he found himself. Warwick's death might set Rey wholeheartedly against his boss, but it certainly presented Lancing with more, and much deadlier problems than he had been prepared for. His previous fears lest Wilder intended to kill him had been tempered by the hope that, when it came to the crunch, the haul from the vault would be enough to satisfy him. Now, he was not so sure. Unless Wilder had an elaborate and foolproof escape route at his disposal, he could scarcely be expected to leave behind any witness who might help convict him for murder.

'Did you get what you wanted?' Rey was standing by the window with his foot on the arm of a chair.

Wilder held the canvas bag above his head and grinned.

'All present and correct,' he said.

'*All* of it?' There was a slight edge to Rey's voice.

'I found all the papers my boss sent me for,' Wilder answered carefully. 'Now we can start to wind up the job. There's no point in hanging around until after dark. We can go out one at a time and . . .'

'Wait a minute. Where's the other guy?' Rey cut in.

'Forget him. All we need to worry about is which direction we intend to take once we get out of here.'

'Stuff it, Wilder. Where the hell's Warwick?'

Wilder took a deep breath and let it out again in an exaggerated sigh.

'You can thank your friend, here, for messing up that little part of the plan,' he said with contempt. 'Tell him, Craven. Tell him what you did to the poor bastard.'

Lancing edged his way to the high-backed chair. His hands had been retied the moment he had stepped from the car, and already the skin around his wrists was beginning to burn. Across from him, Shirley was slumped at one end of the sofa, oblivious to what was going on around her, but a glance at Catherine's ashen face told him that she already knew that George Warwick was dead.

'Where *is* he?' Rey demanded.

Joe Craven spread his hands and shrugged apologetically.

'I had to hit him, Kev. How the hell was I to know that he had some kind of condition? He folded up and couldn't breathe properly, and he was getting worse all the time . . .'

'Well, come on, tell me what happened to him.'

'Get on with it,' Wilder said sharply, annoyed by Craven's hesitation.

'All right. All right.' Some of the cockiness had gone from Craven's voice. 'There was some kind of fight or something out in the street. Vince told me to stay downstairs with the old man, and to keep him quiet. Honestly, Kev, he was making a lot of noise. I was scared they'd hear him from the street so I shut him in the vault.'

Lancing couldn't see Rey's face, but he guessed that his usual deadpan expression would be changed by Craven's story.

'You . . . locked . . . him . . . in . . . the . . . vault?' Rey's voice was cold and deliberate. He left long pauses between each word, as if talking to a very young child or a half-wit.

'That's right.' Craven shrugged again.

'The door has an automatic lock,' Wilder explained, 'and we couldn't find the damn key. There was no way to get him out.'

'Did you try?'

'Of course I did.'

'The poor bastard . . .'

'He's dead,' Wilder said flatly. 'If he wasn't when we left him, he certainly is now. He could hardly breathe. Craven hit him once, and he couldn't even stand without help.'

Rey turned to Lancing. Surprisingly, his face registered neither shock nor anger, though both emotions were evident in his voice.

'Is that how it was?' he asked. 'An accident?'

'A careless accident,' Lancing confirmed. 'The vault is air-tight, and he was already semi-conscious. There was simply no way to get him out . . . no way at all . . . not without the key.'

'Why'd you have to hit him in the first place?' Rey demanded of Craven, but before the younger man could answer, Wilder stepped between them.

'Look, Rey, what's done is done. I didn't want this to happen, any more than you did, but it's *done*, and asking questions won't make things any different.'

'So, now it's murder, just like that?' Rey snapped his fingers in the air close to Wilder's face.

'The boss'll look after us,' Craven interrupted. 'The Big Boss, remember?'

'Balls,' Rey hissed.

'And what's that supposed to mean?' Wilder polished his shotgun with a handkerchief to remove all traces of the finger-prints he had left on the smooth metal. The fact that it was loaded and aimed at Rey's chest seemed not to worry him in the slightest.

'You didn't need any "Big Boss" to pull this job,' Rey said, evenly.

Craven laughed aloud. 'Sure he did, Kev. You heard what he said about the syndicate and how they organized all this to get those papers. He made a telephone call from the shop when he couldn't get in the vault. He had to report back to the boss. He's taking orders, just like we are.'

Rey was shaking his head slowly, still watching Wilder.

'Maybe it wasn't his boss he spoke to,' he suggested. 'Maybe he doesn't *have* a boss.'

'Who the hell was it, then?'

'A contact. That's all he needed, just one contact who was so damn misinformed that he didn't warn him about the time-lock. Right, Vince?'

Lancing looked from one man to the other. Both were smiling, both confident that they had nothing to lose from the confrontation. At last, Wilder's grin widened and he touched the other man's chest very lightly with the shotgun.

'You'll never know, will you, Kevin?'

Without giving Rey time to reply, he glanced at Craven and raised a hand for silence.

'Let's wind the job up, shall we, Kevin? We can talk it over later.' His manner and his tone implied that he wanted Craven out of the way before he discussed the matter further.

Rey nodded his head. He seemed to accept Wilder's words and the promise behind them.

To Lancing, the whole thing was transparent. Wilder was playing for time. Now that the risks involved had increased, it would be interesting to see how the gang leader handled his men. What Rey had said about the contact was quite believable. Perhaps there was no all-powerful boss behind the job. Perhaps all Wilder had was a contact, someone who simply knew when there was something in the vault worth taking. Trump card or bluff, that's what Rey had called Wilder's talk of syndicate connections, but in a game with such high stakes, it would take a real gambling man to demand to see Wilder's hand. As he contemplated the odds against him, Lancing realized that, if Rey failed to force Wilder's hand, sheer desperation would eventually force him to take that chance himself.

While his companions used the top of the desk on which to divide the money which had been taken from the backroom safe, Joe Craven moved round behind the sofa and ran the backs of his fingers first across Shirley's cheek, then across Catherine's. He grinned at Lancing, his lips twisted in cruel pleasure.

Lancing forced himself to lower his head. He suspected that Craven's actions were solely for his benefit, and that he would leave the women alone if his taunts met with no response. He raised his head again almost immediately when Catherine issued a tight little cry. Craven had grabbed a handful of her hair, and was holding her head back at an awkward angle. The big, wide-bladed knife was in his other hand, its cutting edge close to her face.

'I could slit her throat as easy as slicing through an apple,' he sneered. With one flick of his wrist, he cut through the tuft of hair he was holding, then held it up to the light and laughed aloud.

'Take it easy, will you, Craven?' There was a warning note in Rey's voice, but he made no further attempt to prevent Craven from interfering with the women.

Craven tossed the handful of hair above his head and bellowed with laughter as the fair strands scattered in all directions. He blew some from his face, and brushed others from his clothes, and for a moment it seemed that he might repeat the process. Instead, he dipped his calloused hand inside the collar of Shirley's jacket. He jerked it back again with a sharp intake of breath, and the grin vanished from his face. The skin on the back of his hand had been deeply scratched by the twisted paperclip which was holding the two sides of Shirley's jacket together. He ripped the clip free and tossed it across the room, then stood sucking his wound and staring down at her exposed breasts.

Lancing steeled himself to remain silent when Craven twisted his fingers in Shirley's hair and lifted her to her feet. Above the gag, her eyes were tightly closed. Her struggles resulted in a savage tightening of the grip on her hair.

Rey attracted Wilder's attention by prodding his arm and nodding in Craven's direction. Wilder looked round briefly, then checked his watch and casually shrugged his shoulders. He was no longer concerned with how the younger man spent his time, so long as he caused no trouble.

'Stop him,' Lancing shouted, in spite of his concentrated efforts to maintain his self-control. 'For Christ's sake, stop the bastard.'

Craven's fist shot out and landed a blow to his temple which almost knocked him from his chair.

'Stuff you, Lancing,' he grinned, then pulled his victim towards the bedroom without a backward glance.

'What're you going to do about him?' Rey asked, when the bedroom door had slammed behind Craven.

'I'm going to pay him off, just as we agreed when he came in. Have you any other ideas?'

Rey shrugged, dropped into an armchair and draped one leg loosely over its arm.

'I think you should offer him more,' he said. 'That way, he's more inclined to keep out of sight until we're absolutely clear. He could blow this job wide open within five minutes of leaving the house, unless he has a solid gold reason for doing exactly as he's told.'

'Don't worry,' Wilder assured him. 'I'll make sure he stays out of trouble, at least until we're all safely out of this.'

After a long pause, Rey said thoughtfully, 'His chances of staying on the outside don't amount to much, do they?'

'No.' The answer was firm and economical.

'His prints are all over . . . in the shop, the vault, here in the house . . .'

133

'So are yours,' Wilder reminded him.

'But I don't have a police record.'

Wilder nodded. 'How come you've gone all sentimental over Craven, all of a sudden?'

'Maybe I just don't like to see a man taken for a patsy. He might be a crud, but he's sure as hell going to pay for it, isn't he?'

Wilder sat back in a chair and surveyed Rey above his clasped fingers.

'Listen to me,' he said. 'Craven knew the score when he came in on this job. He knew about the guns, yet he chose to be careless about his fingerprints. He's well aware of how it will be for him, with his record, if he gets picked up for a job like this. And what about George Warwick?'

He spread his fingers and smiled, shaking his head gently from side to side.

'Sheer carelessness, Kevin,' he said. 'We're not his nurse-maids. If he chooses to take stupid risks, then he'll just have to accept the consequences.'

'And it works out the same for us, so long as he doesn't blow the whistle on us first.'

'He won't. My boss'll see to that.'

Rey lifted one eyebrow as he studied Wilder's face.

'You're a hard bastard, Wilder,' he observed, not without some measure of admiration.

The other man smiled and tapped his fingers against his teeth.

'That's why I'm running the show, while Craven's only third man,' he said, smugly.

'Leaving me as piggy in the middle?'

Lancing did not enjoy the silence which left Rey's question hanging in the air. Without the conversation of the other two men to distract him, he found his imagination creating un-wanted details about what might be happening in the bedroom. The only alternative to these seemed to be images of George Warwick's death, which brought him out in a cold sweat. He twisted his wrists until his bonds bit deeply into the tender flesh, making him wince with pain. The blisters he rubbed on his skin were effective in keeping his mind clear of uncomfortable thoughts.

Twenty minutes later, Craven swaggered back into the room with a cigarette dangling from a corner of his mouth. He was wearing one of Lancing's sweaters, and Shirley's diamond and ruby ring glittered on the little finger of his left hand. He sneered at Lancing, curling his upper lip over his teeth. He had a self-satisfied look on his face and his eyes were bright. He was bouncing slightly on his toes, tense and breathless, as if still in a state of high excitement.

'You can go, now,' Wilder told him. 'Here's just over six thousand in cash, and I slipped a few extra pieces of jewellery in your bag along with the rest of your stuff. In exactly four hours, you'll be contacted with another ten thousand.'

'Ten? Hey, that's great. I only expected another six.'

Wilder smiled and extended his hand.

'Glad to have had you along,' he said, smoothly. 'Maybe we'll work together again, sometime.'

'Hope so. You sure your contact knows where to find me with the extra cash?'

'He knows,' Wilder assured him. 'Just go directly to the hotel and stay there until you're contacted. My boss will appreciate the way the job worked out.'

'Maybe he'll want to use me again?'

'I'm sure he will,' Wilder smiled. 'Now, get to that hotel, and keep your head down for the next four hours.'

Craven gathered up his bag and made sure that the handle of his knife was concealed beneath the sweater he wore. He shook hands with Rey, oblivious of the coldness in the man's grey eyes. Then he pulled a handful of soft, auburn hair from his pocket and tossed it in Lancing's face.

'A souvenir,' he laughed.

'Bastard!'

'Temper, temper. That's a nice little tart you have there. Christ, I really enjoyed screwing your tart.'

He was still laughing as he slammed the outer door behind him.

'I'm going to kill you, Craven, you bastard,' Lancing yelled after him. 'If it's the last thing I do, I'll find you and I'll kill you.'

His voice was silenced by the threatening closeness of Rey's gun, but the words were still ringing in his head as he heard the hired car pull noisily away from the house.

seventeen

Kevin Rey lifted his jacket from the back of the chair where it had been hanging, and shook it vigorously before pulling it on. He adjusted the cuffs and collar, then smoothed down the lapels. He used his fingers as a comb, scratching them over his head in even strokes. The thick, light brown hair sprang back into place, unaffected by his efforts to tidy it. He checked his pockets, pausing to scowl at his passport as if something about it bothered him. The forged police ID card flickered casually from his fingers and fell to the floor near his feet, where its printed details caught Lancing's eye.

Lancing smiled bitterly to himself. The whole affair would have had a vastly different outcome if he had paid more attention to that card, right at the start. It had been only a few inches from his face, and open to close scrutiny, but his frustration in having his love-making with Shirley interrupted had made him unforgivably careless. Looking at it now, even from a distance, it was painfully obvious to him that the thing was a forgery.

He cleared his throat and looked at the neatly-clipped line where Rey's hair joined the back of his neck.

'Will somebody please make sure that Shirley's all right?' he asked.

Wilder looked at him briefly, but did not acknowledge the question.

136

'Please,' Lancing repeated, aiming his words at Rey. 'Check on her, will you?'

'Why don't you keep your mouth shut for a while, Lancing?' Rey retorted, unexpectedly. 'You're beginning to get on my nerves.'

'But what about Shirley?'

'Stuff it, Lancing.' The words were sharp and final.

Lancing fell silent and tried to convince himself that Shirley was better off in the bedroom now that Craven had gone. At least she was free of the presence of the gang and the constant threat of the guns. He refused to consider the possibility that she was to remain upstairs for the benefit of Wilder or Rey.

The gunmen were standing by the window, sharing hurriedly-made coffee and sweet biscuits. Rey seemed restless and impatient, as if ready to leave.

'It's time you came across with my cut,' he said, through a mouthful of food. 'I'm about ready to get the hell away from here.'

Wilder smiled and set down his coffee cup. He took out a fresh toothpick, dropping several others to the carpet as he did so, and scraped his teeth thoughtfully before reaching into his canvas bag and pulling out two thick bundles of notes.

'Here's the deal,' he explained. 'Your half of the goods, your share of the shop takings, plus another twenty thousand right here. And these . . .'

He stretched out his hand. Four large, uncut diamonds nestled in his gloved palm.

'These are worth holding on to until you can organize a decent price for them. I'm sure you won't be disappointed in their value.'

Rey stared at the glittering stones. His face gave nothing away, but his hesitation implied that he was dubious about Wilder's offer.

'This is the best I can do,' Wilder assured him. 'I didn't expect to find any cash in the vault, so you're welcome to the twenty thousand. The papers were all I came for.'

Rey looked at the canvas bag, then back at the diamonds.

'Take them,' Wilder said. An edge had crept into his voice.

He clearly found Rey's slow, methodical way of working things out irritating. 'Unless you want me to pass on a complaint to my superiors . . . ?'

Rey frowned slightly before reaching for the diamonds. He turned them over in his hand, unimpressed by their possible value.

'They should make you a tidy profit, so long as you fence them properly.'

Rey nodded his head impatiently.

'If you're not happy about it, Kevin, perhaps I should call my boss?'

Max Lancing was very tense. The action was gradually narrowing down to a confrontation between himself and Wilder, and he wasn't ready. Silently, he willed Rey to stand his ground and call Wilder's bluff.

'Forget it, Wilder,' Rey said, pocketing the stones.

'I could try . . .'

'I said, forget it, will you? All I want is my share, my fair share, that's all.'

'And that's exactly what you've got,' Wilder smiled. 'You're a good man to work with, Kevin, thanks a lot.'

He stretched out his hand again, this time in a gesture of friendship. Rey ignored it.

'I did what I was paid for,' he said, quietly. 'You don't have to pat me on the head like a good boy scout.'

'Just trying to be friendly, that's all, Kevin.'

'Stuff your friendship. All I did was what I was paid to do.' He picked up his gear and went towards the door, where he paused with a frown on his face.

'I need a car.'

'Take the dark green one. The keys are still inside. It's Warwick's, so dump it somewhere out of sight as soon as you can.'

'What about you?'

Wilder smiled comfortably. 'Someone's standing by to pick me up when I give them the word. Good luck, Kevin.'

Rey merely nodded. His eyes flickered momentarily over Lancing's face before he turned on his heel and walked briskly to the front door. His footsteps were loud on the steps outside, then the car door opened and closed and the engine purred into life. Within seconds, the car had turned in the drive and was heading for the main gate.

Lancing leaned back in his chair and groaned inwardly as the sound of the car's engine died away. He was surprised to realize just how much he had been counting on Kevin Rey to extricate him from the mess he was in. It was only when an involuntary movement caused his bonds to rub against a painful blister on the inside of his wrist that his mind fully grasped the seriousness of his position. It was almost pay-off time. If Wilder was what he assessed him to be, he would derive a great deal of pleasure from blasting a hole in the head of the man he hated. On the other hand, given the same circumstances, Lancing himself could have been persuaded to forgo even that satisfaction, if the price was right.

His eyes snapped open and looked directly into those of the man who had set himself up as his enemy. Wilder's elbow was propped on the arm of his chair and his cheek rested lightly against his hand. A long, gloved finger made tiny stroking movements across the skin at one corner of his mouth. His smile was lop-sided, his eyes creased with amusement.

'I've beaten you, Lancing,' he said quietly. 'In spite of all your money and your influence, I've walked into your life and ruined you. I've made myself a rich man at your expense, with no comebacks whatsoever. Nobody knows enough about me to put the police on my tail, not even you. You don't even know my real name or my country of origin. Believe me, I have everything worked out to the last detail. When this job is finished, Vince Wilder disappears and I can really start living.'

Lancing breathed steadily and said nothing. He was thinking about the soft leather gloves and the fact that no trace of Wilder would be left behind.

'What about Rey and Craven?' he asked dryly.

Wilder sighed deeply and flicked imaginary bits of dust from his jacket with the backs of his fingers.

'Let's put it this way. I certainly don't plan to spend the rest of my life looking over my shoulder to make sure those two are really off my back.'

'No witnesses? Is that what you mean?'

'It's the only way.'

'And what about us . . . Catherine . . . Shirley . . . what about us?'

Wilder spread his hands and smiled almost apologetically, as if the final outcome of the raid was beyond his control.

'He's going to kill us,' Catherine suddenly said in a tight voice. 'He's going to kill us all, then walk away as if nothing's happened.'

'Shut up,' Lancing snapped. 'How about it, Wilder? Is that your plan? Listen, you don't have to kill me. I can give you enough inside information to organize a dozen jobs like this one. I have contacts . . . influence. With my help you could . . .'

Catherine threw back her head and laughed hysterically. Then she covered her mouth with her hands and allowed the tears to run down her face. Her body shook with sobs, but the noises she made still resembled laughter.

'Two of a kind,' she said, at last, her words muffled by her fingers. 'Two rats . . . both the same . . . rats . . . rats . . .'

'Shut up,' Lancing snapped.

'What kind of men are you? You . . .' she flung at Wilder, '. . . are prepared to betray even those who have helped you. And you . . .' Her eyes narrowed as she turned back on her husband. 'You'll bargain for your own life and not care a damn who might get hurt in the process. He's going to kill us . . . don't you understand? . . . he's going to kill us *all.*'

She covered her face with her hands and collapsed, sobbing, against the back of the sofa.

Lancing tried unsuccessfully to moisten his dry lips. He looked steadily at Wilder, who seemed amused by Catherine's outburst.

'It's not necessary, Vince,' he said, deliberately using the more familiar name. 'We can come to some arrangement. Name your price. Anything you say.'

Wilder lowered his head and surveyed Lancing through his dark lashes. A smile tugged at one corner of his mouth.

'Anything?'

140

Lancing swallowed the lump in his throat and repeated, softly, 'Anything.'

Wilder pushed himself from the chair with exaggerated effort and crossed to the wall mirror to make sure that his teeth were clean and his hair tidy.

'What about it, Vince?' Lancing repeated, trying to keep his voice calm. He wasn't beaten yet. He was still convinced that he could handle Wilder, so long as he stayed calm and planned all his moves meticulously.

As Wilder moved back to the window, Lancing noticed something out of the corner of his eye. Another shape had been momentarily reflected in the mirror, a quick, dark shape which darted across the doorway behind him. An icy coldness made him shudder even as he realized that he was sweating.

Wilder perched himself on the arm of a chair and removed his glove so that he could examine the fingernails of one hand. Even when Lancing could feel the presence of another man close behind him, the gunman's glossy brown head remained lowered. It was Catherine's sudden gasp of surprise which came as a late, but effective, warning.

Wilder's head shot up and his eyes widened before narrowing into menacing slits.

'Well, well, well,' he said casually, as he slowly replaced his glove. His initial surprise was almost instantly concealed by his wide, easy smile.

'I'm not happy about it, Wilder.' It was Rey's voice. He was standing behind Lancing's chair, and the barrel of his pistol was very close to the side of Lancing's head.

'So, what is it you're after?' Wilder asked. 'How come you feel you have to creep in here through the back door?'

'I don't trust you.' The statement was flat, emotionless.

'You could have said that before you left. Why the elaborate pretence? You must have intended coming back, or you wouldn't have taken the trouble to open the side door.'

'I wasn't sure,' Rey said. 'There wasn't enough time for me to get it all clear in my mind. I just wanted to make certain that I could get back inside if I needed to.'

141

'And here you are,' Wilder smiled.

Lancing wondered if he was trying to make a guess at how long Rey had been in the house, and how much he had heard of Wilder's plans.

'All I want is a fair share,' Rey insisted.

'That's what you already have, Kevin.'

'I'm not sure. I don't like this whole set-up. You've very likely got me ear-marked by the big boss, and I didn't ask for that. You've got me involved in murder, and I didn't ask for that, either. I don't have the cash or the contacts to get myself out of this mess, Wilder, and I don't feel happy about you pulling my strings.'

'How long have you been in the house?' Lancing blurted. 'Did you hear him say he wanted no witnesses, not even you and Craven? He intends killing us and throwing you two to the wolves.'

'That's what I figured.' Rey moved further into the room, his big hand steady as it held the pistol.

Wilder glanced at Lancing, unperturbed by his outburst. He was still perched on the arm of the chair. He seemed relaxed, even with Rey's bulk looming over him, even though he was looking into the barrel of a loaded gun. His shotgun lay on the desk just a few feet away, uselessly out of reach.

'So, what do you suggest, Kevin? What exactly did you come back for?'

'Half of what's in there,' Rey said, indicating the white canvas bag.

'That wouldn't be very wise . . .'

'I'll negotiate. You tell your boss that all I want is a fair deal. Those papers are no use to me. I don't even need to know what they are. All I want is what I'm entitled to so you tell that boss of yours that I'm willing to negotiate.'

'Now be reasonable, Kevin . . .'

The finger on the trigger of the pistol tightened and the barrel lifted so that it was in line with Wilder's chest.

'No more dealing with you, Wilder. Give me half those papers, and tell your boss that I deal only with him from now on. Murder makes it a bigger deal, and I want my fair share.'

'This is stupid, Kevin.'

'Just do it,' Rey ordered.

Lancing was keyed up with excitement. He could have told Rey about the diamonds and the cash, but he wanted to see Wilder's bluff through to the bitter end.

Wilder shrugged his shoulders and got to his feet, moving slowly, determined to maintain the deception. The canvas bag lay on the small table near the bookcase. He paused as his fingers touched the neatly-bound drawstring.

'Are you sure this is what you want?'

'I'm certain.'

'It means you'll be putting yourself on the wrong side of some pretty tough people.'

Rey jerked the gun slightly and made no answer.

'Look, let's sit down and work something out,' Wilder coaxed. 'It doesn't have to be like this.'

Lancing stared from one man to the other. Both were calm, but a pulse throbbed steadily in Wilder's neck, and the handsome dark face showed the merest trace of tension. He wondered if Wilder was sweating beneath the expensive clothes.

'Just hand over the papers, Wilder, and forget the dialogue.'

'If you insist . . .'

'Do it!'

Lancing watched Wilder's left hand lift the bag, saw his other hand slip inside, and in one agonizing flash of realization, knew that he was reaching for the pistol he had found in the vault. Before the cry of warning even left his lips the bottom of the bag ripped open and Kevin Rey's muscular chest was shattered by three rapidly fired shots.

eighteen

The gunman's body jerked grotesquely as each bullet tore into him with deadly and almost silent accuracy. He staggered back against the wall at the side of the desk, clutching his chest. When he fell to the floor, part of the bookcase toppled with him, scattering books and ornaments around his body. He fell on his back, his jacket gaping open to reveal the bloody holes in his shirt. Only seconds after the shots, his body was without movement save for the glistening flow of blood on the carpet.

Lancing felt his heart pounding against his ribs as he gaped at the dead man. The cold grey eyes were staring at the ceiling, the mouth slightly open. Death had come too suddenly to allow a cry to push itself from his lips, but the horror of what was happening to him had registered on his features. For the first time, Lancing was able to read the expression on the man's face.

Vince Wilder stood looking down at the body of his colleague. He appeared unmoved, but his gloved hands were tightly clenched, and the strong pulse still throbbed just below his ear. After staring at Rey for a long time, he strode to the kitchen and brought back two hand towels. These he placed very carefully over Rey's head and chest. Then he flopped into an armchair and stared at the wall before him, his face closed.

'You overplayed your hand, Lancing,' he said at last. 'You were so damn eager to tell him what a bad risk I was, that you forgot about the gun.'

'I didn't think you'd kill him . . .'

'You just wanted to set the cat among the pigeons, I suppose. Well, it didn't work, Lancing. All you succeeded in doing was getting Rey killed and making me mad.'

'You can't blame me for trying, Vince. You'd have done the same thing yourself.'

'Stuff it, Lancing. And tell that wife of yours to stop snivelling.'

Lancing was surprised to see that spots of Rey's blood had

144

stained the light silk of Catherine's dressing-gown. She wept against her hands, her features contorted and her sobs making harsh rasping noises in the back of her throat. Her head was turned so that he could see the patch of scalp from which Craven had hacked a wide tuft of hair.

'Hush, Catherine,' he said instinctively, and he suddenly ached with a desire to take her in his arms and hold her against him, to offer, and perhaps receive, a little comfort from the fear which circumstances had provoked in them both. Then he remembered that he was fighting for his life. If he was going to get anything at all from Wilder, it could only be on equal terms. Hard as the gunman was, Lancing knew that he must match him, step by step and mood by mood. When Catherine made no noticeable attempt to pull herself together, Lancing hid his own fear behind the sharpness of his voice.

'Shut up, Catherine. Hold your tongue, dammit.'

Wilder reached into his inside jacket pocket and withdrew his hand slowly, smiling as he revealed the small, leather-bound book which he had taken from the vault.

'Things kept behind locked doors have always intrigued me,' he said. Then he made himself comfortable in his chair and proceeded to read each page in silence.

Lancing watched his face, saw one dark brow raise from time to time in interest or surprise. His gloved hand turned each page awkwardly, while the expression on his face showed that he was impressed by what he read.

'Well, well, well,' he murmured, crossing his legs at the ankles as he reached the last page. He nipped the bridge of his nose with his finger and thumb and sat for a while in silence, his eyes closed and his tongue protruding slightly from between his teeth.

'Well, well, well,' he repeated, some time later. 'Very interesting. Very interesting indeed. Tell me, Mrs Lancing, have you any idea just what your husband is into?'

Catherine shook her head, her face ashen and her eyes red and swollen from weeping. She twisted nervously at her handkerchief with both hands.

'Shall I tell you what's in this book, lady?' Wilder waved the book in the air. 'It contains details of all the illegal diamond trading that's been going on for years behind the scenes in that innocent-looking shop. I could use this information to put a whole crowd of rich and powerful people behind bars for a long time, and your louse of a husband would be first in the queue.'

Catherine closed her eyes and shuddered, but made no reply.

'It's over, lady,' Wilder said with a sneer. 'The good life is all over for you. I'm taking *everything*.'

He looked at Lancing and smiled as he tapped one corner of the book against the top of his extended fingers.

'It goes to the highest bidder, Lancing, and it doesn't matter to me if that's a client, a cop, or an outsider with a stomach for blackmail. You've already made me a very rich man, my friend, and when this little item goes on the open market, I'll be even richer.'

Lancing swallowed the lump in his throat. He shivered violently, in spite of the pockets of sweat on his body. Wilder didn't need to kill him. He could get the job done without even having to ask. All he had to do was use the book and make the source of his information known to any one of a dozen men named in it.

'I might kill you, Lancing,' Wilder announced unexpectedly, lifting the shotgun so that it pointed at Lancing's head.

'If I get rid of you and your wife, I can walk out of here a free man. There'll only be Craven left . . . oh, yes . . . and your little lady upstairs. But what could either of them tell the police about me?'

Lancing licked his lips and tried to clear his mind. Something like panic was welling up in him.

'The book,' he almost yelled. 'What about the book?' He no longer cared about the note of desperation which he heard in his own voice. He didn't want to die. 'I'll give you half a million . . . cash . . . for the book.'

'Balls.' Wilder smiled.

'I have it . . . in my Swiss account . . . it's yours . . . for the book.' Lancing's voice was hoarse. He had just dealt his last card. 'Half a million . . . cash . . .'

146

Instead of answering Lancing, Wilder nudged Catherine's shoulder and spoke to her sharply.

'I need a fresh bag. This one's ripped.'

'In the back room just off the hall, next to the lavatory. Left-hand shelf.' Catherine's voice was a dull monotone. There seemed barely a spark of spirit remaining in her.

Lancing watched Wilder walk casually from the room and down the hall. To his amazement, Catherine leaped from her seat the moment the gunman was out of sight. She darted to the body of Kevin Rey, snatched the pistol from beneath his leg, and returned to her seat in a matter of seconds. She pushed the weapon behind a small cushion which had become crushed in a corner of the sofa. Lancing was cheered by her quick thinking and courage, though he doubted that she would be capable of pulling the trigger. Even in her haste to secure it, she had used her handkerchief rather than allow the bloodied metal to touch her fingers. By the time Vince Wilder walked back into the room just a few seconds later, she was sitting as he had seen her last, hunched and silent.

Wilder transferred the money to the small leather bag and covered it with the velvet-lined box containing the diamonds. When he realized that this would leave insufficient room for his shotgun, he tipped the stones into his handkerchief and put them in his jacket pocket.

'Rey was right, you know,' he said. 'I didn't need a boss on this job. All I needed was a contact to tell me the best time to make my move. Think about that, Lancing.' He looked at his watch and nodded his head, then, holding his shotgun loosely under one arm, picked up the telephone and dialled a number.

'Got any ideas, Lancing, about who the contact might be? Don't let the telephone call fool you. This is personal. The contact is a bit closer to home . . . Hi there, guess who?'

As he smiled into the receiver, Catherine Lancing's hand slid beneath the cushion.

'We made it,' Wilder laughed. 'More than we expected, and even more to come. We made it.'

Lancing saw the barrel of the pistol emerge from behind the cushion. He hardly dared breathe in case the sound distracted

147

Wilder from his conversation. He stared at the gunman's face, and when he looked back at his wife, she was sitting with the gun in her hand. It was aimed at Wilder's partly turned back, and though its handle was still covered by the handkerchief, the small, neatly manicured hand which gripped it was surprisingly steady.

'Have you got the car ready?' Wilder spoke into the mouthpiece. 'Good, good. I want you to come and pick me up. Make sure you've got everything. I don't want to have to make any stops between here and the plane.'

He shifted the shotgun as he spoke, rocking it gently in his hand as if testing its weight.

'Now here's the address. Get here as soon as you can so that . . .'

Wilder's whole body suddenly stiffened and his mouth fell open as he caught sight of Catherine Lancing with the pistol in her hand.

'Vince? Vince? Is there anything wrong?' The small voice on the other end of the telephone line was the only sound in the room.

Wilder's shotgun was pointing at the floor. Lancing watched it start to swing in a wide arc, its deadly barrel moving towards Catherine. He saw Wilder's finger already beginning to squeeze the trigger, and he knew, in that instant, that if Catherine didn't kill him, they would all die.

The heavy pistol jerked with a single shot which slammed into Wilder's body just below his ribs. He sank to the floor, clutching his torn flesh with one hand and his shotgun with the other. He scuttled backwards across the carpet, as if trying to escape the pain of his injury. When his back made contact with the bookshelves at the other side of the room, he pulled his feet close to his body and tried to stand.

Catherine slowly got to her feet and stared at the blood which oozed out between Wilder's fingers, made worse by his persistent efforts to stand. She watched him slump back into a sitting position, unable to summon any more strength, unable even to raise the shotgun which lay on the blood-smeared carpet beneath his right hand.

Lancing's muscles relaxed to the point of weakness as relief washed over him like a wave of nausea. Almost immediately, he began to tremble, but at the same time, his mind became crystal clear.

'Untie me,' he said, sharply. 'Get this damn necktie off my wrists.'

It was all over. He had beaten Wilder, after all. Now he had to hide the book and the cash. He had to get the diamonds from Wilder's pocket and into a safe place. There was a lot to do before he could call in the police. He would tell them that the gang had been after the jewellery and legitimate cash which was kept in the shop, and that they decided to raid his home when they found the vault empty. He had to cover himself, get his story clear in his mind before the police came to ask him questions.

'Untie me, Catherine,' he repeated, more sharply this time. He managed to get to his feet, turned his back, and pushed his hands towards her.

'For God's sake, Catherine. Wake up!'

She dropped the pistol and fumbled with the necktie which bound his wrists. She was crying and laughing at the same time.

Wilder watched them through half-closed eyes, his face very calm. His breathing was so shallow as to be almost imperceptible. Blood soaked into his clothes and stained the carpet and some of the furniture around him. His glove had soaked up so much blood that it blended with the crimson mass of his wound, making it difficult to tell where the glove ended and the injury began. It didn't really matter what other damage the close-range bullet had done to his insides. He was bleeding to death.

Lancing wriggled his hands impatiently, angered by Catherine's fumbling fingers and her hoarse sobbing. Already, the details of the story he would give to the police were coming together in his mind. He was still trembling and agitated, so highly excited that he could have bellowed with laughter or dropped to his knees and wept. As the necktie fell away from his wrists, he turned swiftly and quietened Catherine's sobs with a flat-handed blow to her face which almost knocked her down. His action shocked her into silence, and at the same time brought a measure of relief to his own pent-up emotions. He reached out to steady her, but she shook her arm free of his grip and glared at him through large, accusing eyes.

'Now, you listen to me,' he said, firmly. 'I want you to stay calm and pay attention to everything I say to you. Wait here while I fetch Shirley, then we'll work out a story to tell the police. All right?'

She stared at him without blinking her eyes.

'Answer me!' He yelled so loudly that her body jolted and a small cry escaped from her lips.

'All right,' she whispered. 'I'll do as you say.'

'I'll get Shirley,' he repeated, almost tripping over Wilder's outstretched legs as he made for the door.

'Max . . . Max . . .' Catherine's voice was strained.

Lancing ignored her. She was practically distraught, and hysteria was the last thing he felt capable of dealing with at that time.

He took the steps two at a time and flung open the door of the master bedroom. Both beds had been used. The covers of one of them had been pulled to the floor and left in an untidy heap. The contents of the long wardrobe were strewn about the room and all the drawers were hanging open, their items scattered. There was no sign of Shirley.

He turned towards the guest room and stopped in his tracks, staring at the partly-open door. Craven's jacket and T-shirt lay on the carpet just outside the door. He gaped at them, transfixed by the stains they had left on the pale carpet. They were saturated with blood.

He moved slowly forward and allowed his extended hand to push gently against the door. It opened slowly and smoothly before him. He stood, numbed, drained of all physical sensation, staring into the room.

Shirley Foster lay spread-eagled across the bed, naked save for the remnants of her jacket and the lace suspender belt around her waist. Her head lolled back over the edge of the mattress, and her eyes seemed to stare straight into Lancing's face. What was left of her hair hung down into the dark, moist stain on the carpet. Her throat had been cut.

nineteen

Lancing leaned his head against the door frame and closed his eyes. He was aware of his own heartbeat and the sound of his breath as he sucked it through clenched teeth. A hot tear squeezed itself from behind the lid of his left eye and rolled down his cheek to the corner of his mouth. He licked it away with his tongue and grimaced at its saltiness. When he opened his eyes again, his gaze fell on a sheer stocking which lay on the floor just inside the room. Part of a fastener still clung to its silky top, torn from the belt by an impatient hand. Lancing allowed the stocking to slip through his fingers. It snagged on a broken fingernail and hung there until he shook it free.

He turned from the room and walked to the top of the stairs. When his hand touched the banister, he gripped it tightly until his knuckles whitened under the strain. He walked unsteadily down the stairs. He was suddenly very weary.

'She's dead,' he said, as he entered the sitting-room. His own voice sounded strange to him, his words meaningless.

'She's dead,' he repeated. 'He killed her. The bastard killed her.'

He picked up the telephone and fumbled with the dial. He struggled to penetrate the numbness which enveloped him and gradually a sense of reality began to return to him.

The receiver was silent against his ear. He pressed his hand on the cradle and dialled again, muttering each number as he did so. When there was still no response from the instrument, he picked it up and slammed it down on the arm of the nearest chair, frustration causing him to grind his teeth together. It

151

was only when he brought the receiver back to his ear that his shocked senses registered the fact that the telephone was dead. He tugged at the wire. It snaked across the carpet towards him, its ends exposed where they had been ripped from the wall. He had a sudden and very clear mental picture of Wilder dropping the receiver as he fell, leaving the person to whom he had been speaking yelling into the mouthpiece on the other end of the line. The telephone had not been damaged when Wilder was shot. It must have been torn from the wall when Lancing was upstairs.

He turned to look at his wife, the loose wire hanging limply from his fingers. She was staring back at him, her eyes steady and her lips pulled into a tight, bitter line.

'Catherine?' His gaze travelled from her face to the shot-gun in her hand. The trigger and part of the handle were covered by the large handkerchief she was holding. There was no blood on the shotgun, no reason why she should protect her hand from it. When he looked at Kevin Rey, he saw that his pistol had been returned to his hand and his lifeless fingers bent around its handle.

'Catherine?' he stammered. 'I don't understand . . .'

She smiled coldly and reached down without taking her eyes from his face.

'Sit down, Max.'

He sat down heavily in the opposite chair and watched her pick up the small pistol which had once belonged to George Warwick. The clumsy silencer had been removed, and the small weapon was partly concealed by her dressing-gown. There would be no tell-tale fingerprints left behind on the smooth metal. As the pistol came almost level with Lancing's head, she pulled the trigger.

He ducked, instinctively covering his head with his hands as the sound of the shot reverberated round the room and the bullet embedded itself in the wall behind him. Outside, the buzzing of an electric lawnmower stopped abruptly.

'Catherine . . . for God's sake . . .'

She fired again, this time aiming the gun at the window. The

152

glass shattered, and the sound of the shot and the breaking glass seemed to hang on the still air outside the house. Before its echoes had died away, she had hurled the weapon into the farthest corner of the room. At no time did she lower the shotgun, or allow it to falter from its aim at her husband's body.

His ears rang, but Lancing's mind was suddenly, sharply, alert. He looked at Wilder, whose eyes still glittered with life, in spite of the seriousness of his wound.

'You?' he said hoarsely, without looking at her. 'You're the contact he was talking about?'

'The same, Max.'

'But why? Why?'

She laughed aloud, a shrill, humourless sound.

He looked at her now, shocked by the calm hostility he saw in her eyes.

'Revenge?' he asked. 'If that's all you want, Catherine, go upstairs and take a look in the guest room. Shirley's dead. Craven cut her throat. Go up there and see for yourself how she died, if you want revenge so badly.'

'Oh, I'm glad she's dead, Max. At first I hated her, that's why I wanted her to be there when Wilder ruined your business. Then I felt sorry for her, especially after Craven . . . but I'm glad she's dead.'

Lancing licked his lips and moved his hand in Wilder's direction. 'Was he your lover?' he demanded. 'Did he seduce you into betraying me?'

Catherine laughed again and cast a contemptuous glance at the dying gunman before smiling indulgently at her husband.

'Shall I tell you, Max? Shall I tell you how all this came about?'

He nodded cautiously. She was beginning to relax. With care, he should be capable of closing the gap between them and overpowering her. But first her attention would have to be distracted from the shotgun.

'I found him waiting for me one afternoon when I came out of the hairdresser's,' she explained. 'He had accidentally reversed into my car while parking. Nothing serious, just a small

153

scratch and a cracked lamp. He took me to lunch, sent me flowers, rang me . . . it was all very romantic, really.'

Lancing eased himself forward in his chair and placed his feet in such a position that he would be well balanced if the opportunity arose for decisive action. Some way to his right, Vince Wilder still held on to the gaping wound in his belly. He looked weary, but no sign of pain had registered on his handsome face. The forefinger of his right hand picked gently at the tufts in the carpet, as if he needed that small movement to convince himself that he was still alive.

'It didn't take long for me to realize what he was after,' Catherine continued, 'so I played along with him, gave him what information I could. Then, when I heard you and George talking about a new shipment of diamonds which was due to arrive, I told Wilder to go ahead and take it. We were using each other, you see.'

She suddenly scowled angrily. She was no longer looking at her husband. Her eyes were fixed on a point somewhere above his head.

'I never wanted all this,' she said, tightly. 'You were so damn secretive, Max. That's why I didn't know about the time-lock. When Wilder rang me from the shop and told me that he couldn't get inside the vault, I wasn't sure what to do. I couldn't let him fail. Simply robbing the shop would have meant nothing to you . . . your insurance would cover the loss and you'd just go on as before.'

'And you wanted to ruin me, punish me for hurting you?' Lancing spoke gently, trying to show her that he understood her motives for trying to harm him.

She nodded.

'So, that's what this is all about. Plain, old-fashioned revenge.' It was a statement without bitterness, quietly spoken.

'He was to do the job and go away,' she said, her voice a soft monotone. I didn't want all this. In the end, he betrayed me, Max, just as you did. He was going to kill us all.'

'Put the gun down, Cathy.'

'It was so easy to kill him. All I had to do was pull the

154

trigger. How will anyone know it was me? What about Craven? Or you?'

'Please, Cathy, put the gun down.'

Lancing forced himself to smile. Somebody was certain to have reported hearing shots from the house. The police might arrive at any moment to find him sitting there, surrounded by enough incriminating evidence to send him to prison for a good many years.

'They'll put me away, Cathy,' he said. 'The money . . . the diamonds . . . the book . . . they'll put me away. What will you do then? You don't have much money of your own. In Switzerland I have . . .'

'You have *nothing*,' she cut in, bitterly. '*Nothing*. I closed your Swiss number accounts three days ago.'

Lancing's mouth fell open in disbelief. Her words were like a blow in the face.

'You were careless,' she continued. 'You never once suspected that boring, predictable Catherine was capable of playing you at your own game. And what makes you think I'd let them put you in prison, when I stand to gain so much more as your widow?'

'Good God, woman, you can't mean that . . .'

'But my dear, you're very heavily insured.'

Lancing was stunned, fully aware of nothing but her words and the shotgun.

'In the last few hours,' Catherine said, her voice terrifyingly normal, 'I have watched you try to turn every move to your own advantage. When it comes to the crunch, survival is all that matters, isn't it, Max? Wilder didn't intend letting *anything* come between him and his ultimate plans, and neither did you. Well, it's my turn now . . . my turn to win the game.'

The siren of a police car wailed in the distance, coming closer.

'They'll never suspect *me*, Max,' Catherine was saying. 'I'm just an innocent victim, assaulted and humiliated by vicious criminals. But you, Max . . . you were the hero. You tried to fight back, to overpower the gang . . . and you succeeded, my dear. Just look how successful you were. How very unfortunate that you got yourself killed in the process.'

Images flashed through Lancing's mind in quick succession. He saw Rey's chest blown apart by three bullets, Vince Wilder shot at close range, Shirley staring at him with her wide, dead eyes.

'Cathy . . . darling . . . please listen to me . . .'

The piercing sound of the police siren was closer now, high-pitched and penetrating. His eyes were drawn to Wilder, whose finger still picked at the carpet while his half-closed eyes stared towards the centre of the room. There was a pallor about his skin that made his eyes look bright and dark-rimmed. The smell of his blood was rich on the warm air.

'Please, Cathy . . .' Lancing heard himself begging. 'We can go away. We can take everything and make a fresh start. Just the two of us . . . there's still time . . .'

He was suddenly conscious of the stubble and the dried blood on his face, the bruises, the aching muscles, the staleness of his breath. His blistered wrists burned, and the strength of his heartbeat was almost painful in his ears. The tightness in his chest and belly caused a hot, familiar tightness in his groin.

'No deals,' Catherine said.

'Please . . . please . . .'

Over by the bookcase, a soft, liquid sound escaped from Wilder's throat. His lips had pulled back from his teeth. A trickle of blood ran down his chin and dropped on to his shirt.

'I'm going to kill you, Max Lancing,' Catherine whispered.

The siren stopped somewhere along the avenue, then started up again almost immediately, heading towards the house. Lancing imagined a public-spirited neighbour directing the police to the source of the shooting. His heart pounded against his ribs as tyres screeched on the gravelled drive. He could feel perspiration gathering between his toes and down the centre of his back.

'Listen to me, Cathy,' he pleaded. 'We can work as a team. We can take the diamonds and the cash for ourselves . . . sell the book to the highest bidder . . .'

156

He drew himself slowly to his feet and took a hesitant step towards her. His scalp prickled, and his eyes felt as if they were bulging in their sockets. He had never been so agonizingly aware of his own body.

'A fifty-fifty split,' he said. 'From now on, we go all out for everything we can get, and we split it down the middle, equal shares, just you and me. What d'you say, Cathy?'

Catherine stood up suddenly and laughed at her husband's reaction. Her unexpected movement caused him to stiffen nervously. She backed away from him, smiling into his face as if encouraging him to follow her.

Lancing took a deep breath and inched his way towards her.

Outside, a police officer called for the occupants to leave the house along with any firearms they possessed. It was the first step, the official request, designed to protect possible hostages by giving the gunman a chance to surrender peacefully. After a few minutes, he would no doubt radio for reinforcements and the house would be surrounded.

'What d'you say, Cathy?' Lancing repeated.

'What about her? What about Shirley Foster?'

'She's dead,' he reminded her.

'And you never were very good at mourning, were you, Max?' she said with sarcasm.

'We can talk about that . . . give me a chance, Cathy. For God's sake, give me a chance.'

A different voice ordered them to leave the house. Soon, the driveway would be crawling with police and there would be no time left to work anything out.

'Come on, Cathy,' Lancing pleaded, softly. She was no more than a metre away, now, smiling up into his face, the shotgun tilted so that it was aimed at his head. Without taking her eyes from his face, she extended her hand until her fingers touched Wilder's hair.

'No deals, Max.'

'Listen to me, Cathy.' He edged closer, watching her bright eyes. 'After all these years, there must be something left between us. You know I love you.'

He was smiling. He could feel his lips drawn tight across his teeth. He seemed to be aware of every part of his body at the same time. His nostrils flared, irritated by the sickly-sweet smell of Wilder's blood. His hand reached out towards the shotgun.

'How very touching, Max,' she said, evenly.

'I love you,' he repeated, his voice firm and steady. He knew that his life depended on his ability to reach her through her own weakness, her need for love. As the tips of his fingers brushed the smooth metal, his entire body quivered with overwhelming triumph. He had succeeded!

Catherine Lancing returned her husband's smile all the time she was squeezing the trigger. His fingers were already closing round the barrel of the shotgun when she blasted him full in the face.

As the echo of the shot faded, she heard more police cars roar into the driveway and scream to a halt close to the house. She pushed the shotgun back into Wilder's hand and smiled into his ashen face. His lips twitched as his fingers closed around the familiar weapon. It almost seemed as if he, too, was smiling. She looked down at his wound and nodded her head, satisfied that he was very close to death.

She lifted the diamonds from his pocket, held the handkerchief between her finger and thumb, then swung her arm in a wide arc, scattering the sparkling gems around the room. Then she ripped her dressing-gown open and tore the flimsy nightgown beneath. A smile pulled at the corner of her mouth as she touched the large patch on her scalp where Craven's knife had sliced through her hair. She rubbed roughly at her eyes with both fists until tiny coloured lights danced behind her lids and the skin prickled painfully. After examining her reflection in the wall mirror with approval, she took a deep breath and knelt on the floor next to her husband's body, averting her eyes from the mess that had been his face. His blood soaked rapidly into her clothes. She dabbed at it with the handkerchief she had used to prevent her fingerprints being left on the two guns.

Close by, Vince Wilder's fingers moved momentarily on the shotgun before the dark brightness of his eyes became a sightless glaze.

When four heavily-armed policemen burst into the house some time later, they found only Catherine Lancing left alive, slumped over the body of her husband, shocked and incoherent.

Bestselling Fiction and Non-Fiction

☐ **The Amityville Horror**	Jay Anson	80p
☐ **Shadow of the Wolf**	James Barwick	95p
☐ **The Island**	Peter Benchley	£1.25p
☐ **Castle Raven**	Laura Black	£1.25p
☐ **Smart-Aleck Kill**	Raymond Chandler	95p
☐ **Sphinx**	Robin Cook	£1.25p
☐ **The Entity**	Frank De Felitta	£1.25p
☐ **Trial Run**	Dick Francis	95p
☐ **The Rich are Different**	Susan Howatch	£1.95p
☐ **Moviola**	Garson Kanin	£1.50p
☐ **Tinker Tailor Soldier Spy**	John le Carré	£1.50p
☐ **The Empty Copper Sea**	John D. MacDonald	90p
☐ **Where There's Smoke**	Ed McBain	80p
☐ **The Master Mariner**		
Book 1: Running Proud	Nicholas Monsarrat	£1.50p
☐ **Bad Blood**	Richard Neville and	
	Julie Clarke	£1.50p
☐ **Victoria in the Wings**	Jean Plaidy	£1.25p
☐ **Fools Die**	Mario Puzo	£1.50p
☐ **Sunflower**	Marilyn Sharp	95p
☐ **The Throwback**	Tom Sharpe	95p
☐ **Wild Justice**	Wilbur Smith	£1.50p
☐ **That Old Gang of Mine**	Leslie Thomas	£1.25p
☐ **Caldo Largo**	Earl Thompson	£1.50p
☐ **Harvest of the Sun**	E. V. Thompson	£1.25p
☐ **Future Shock**	Alvin Toffler	£1.95p

All these books are available at your local bookshop or newsagent, or can be ordered direct from the publisher. Indicate the number of copies required and fill in the form below

Name_____
(block letters please)

Address_____

_____

Send to Pan Books (CS Department), Cavaye Place, London SW10 9PG
Please enclose remittance to the value of the cover price plus:

25p for the first book plus 10p per copy for each additional book ordered to a maximum charge of £1.05 to cover postage and packing
Applicable only in the UK

While every effort is made to keep prices low, it is sometimes necessary to increase prices at short notice. Pan Books reserve the right to show on covers and charge new retail prices which may differ from those advertised in the text or elsewhere